PERSONAL FOUL

PERSONAL FOUL

LUCY J. MADISON

SAPPHIRE BOOKS

SALINAS, CALIFORNIA

Editor - Nikki Busch
Book Designer - LJ Reynolds
Cover Designer - Michelle Brodeur

Sapphire Books Publishing, LLC
P.O. Box 8142
Salinas, CA 93912
www.sapphirebooks.com

Printed in the United States of America
First Edition – March 2016

This and other Sapphire Books titles can be found at
www.sapphirebooks.com

Dedication

To my wife D. for everything.

Acknowledgments

I am eternally grateful for the creative spirit that resides deep inside me and is always available when called upon. Thank you to Christine Svendsen and the entire team at Sapphire Books Publishing for taking a chance on me and for their hard work and support. To my editor, Nikki Busch, thank you for polishing my words with such care and grace. I hope this is the first of many projects we work on together. Special thanks to the people and places of Provincetown and to the players and referees of the WNBA. Finally, to my best friends and official hangover crew: D., N., M., and C.—here's to another twenty-eight years of laughter and love; the nursing home will be a blast. Consider this as payoff for keeping all my secrets safe and sound. I.V. now and always.

Part One

It is the flash which appears, the thunderbolt will follow.
—Voltaire

Chapter One

Kat Schaefer feels the familiar acceleration as the force pulls her body deeper into the seat. Here she sits in another airplane during another takeoff to another city. She missed her first flight after yet another time-consuming TSA search simply because her ticket was randomly coded, but finally, she can relax. As she prepares to lean back and take a long-awaited nap, Kat glimpses the hand of the older woman next to her and notices she is clutching the armrest.

"I never get used to this," the nervous woman says to Kat almost apologetically.

"It's okay. It will get better in a few minutes once we hit altitude."

"I really hate to fly. I prefer to be in a drug-induced stupor but my daughter wouldn't let me take anything since I'm flying alone."

Kat smiles politely but doesn't feel like talking. She raises the window shade and squints outside. She can feel the Phoenix heat pulsing through the thick double-paned glass. There isn't anything more scorching than Phoenix in late July other than a hot frying pan. After a look into the haze, she closes the window shade and closes her eyes. Trying to adjust her long legs in the cramped space isn't easy; at five foot ten inches tall, Kat has never been completely comfortable in a coach seat. With long, straight black hair, steel-gray eyes, and an athletic, tall build, Kat Schaefer is strikingly beautiful and usually, both men and women turn their heads when she walks by. They also tend to talk to her on planes and in airports when she'd much rather remain anonymous.

For a split second, Kat can't even remember what city she is headed to, but then she remembers she's on her way home. She worked a game in Phoenix last night and a game in Minneapolis the night before that. She remembers that much. Professional officials in the Women's National Basketball Association, or WNBA, aren't supposed to have favorites, but Kat loves working Diana Taurasi's games. Sometimes the games run into each other, with little differentiating one night from another, but when Taurasi plays, she, at least, makes things interesting; her bubbly and highly competitive personality helps break up the monotony of the game. Last night was a close game, but thankfully, it was won by the play on the court and not by an official's call. Now, Kat is headed home for few days off. She prefers traveling from hotel to hotel rather than spending any time in her home, but sometimes going home isn't something she can opt out of.

As she allows the familiar hiss and drone of the plane to relax her, she tries not to let her mind wander to Danielle. It's better not to think of her at all, Kat muses as if she still needs convincing that their life together is over.

After the NCAA season ended last March, Kat returned home exhausted to a nearly empty house. She still painfully remembers the echoing sound her shoes made as she walked across the hardwood floor of the living room. *Their* living room. The house they bought together in Westchester just north of New York City after being together for a year. The furniture they picked out and then made love on the same night it was delivered to "break it in" was all gone. All of it. Seven years of a relationship gone down the drain too. Danielle left only Kat's personal belongings along with a note that read:

Kat: I can no longer be the only one in this relationship anymore. I'm tired of being alone and found someone who wants to be with me, really with me. I hope you find happiness in all those empty hotel rooms.

Over a year later, the house that Danielle left her is still empty. Kat can't bring herself to sell it, nor is she home long enough to really let it sink in. In fact, she has stubbornly convinced herself that having less furniture makes the place more spacious and free of any emotional attachments. She still can't quite release the hurt of being left behind yet again, no matter how many air miles she logs.

☙ ☙ ☙ ☙ ☙

Later the same evening, Kat arrives back at her small crème-colored Victorian house in a busy neighborhood. She sizes the house up as she pulls in the driveway. Admittedly, the place has character, at least from the outside. She takes time to unstuff the mailbox that's filled to the brim and immediately notices the hydrangeas along the front walkway are drooping badly in the midsummer heat. Before entering the house, she makes sure to give the plants a good soaking.

An hour later, her oldest and best friend Molly comes over for her second "Come to Jesus" talk in the last month. Molly is a typical Irish girl: red hair, fair skin, a round face dotted with freckles, and rosy cheeks. She's much shorter than Kat, but her big personality makes her seem a lot taller. She works as a vet tech at a large veterinary hospital, a fact Kat always laughs at since Molly never had pets growing up and never showed an ounce of interest in them either. Now, it's a different story. Molly is constantly fostering a pet in need or caring for one at home while it heals from one medical issue or another.

After a few beers and Chinese takeout on the folding table in her dining room, Molly looks around the sparse room and shakes her head while she puts her long red hair up in a ponytail.

"Jesus, Kat, how much longer are you going to live like a monk? This place is fucking depressing. I know you miss her, and I know you lost your bearings for a while, but you need to pull yourself together. It's been over a year. This is the kind of place either a CIA spy or a serial killer lives in."

"Molly, I am together. My life is exactly how I want it. This place is fine for now. You know I'm always on the road, so what difference will a dining room table or a few pictures on the walls make, anyway?"

"First of all, I'd much prefer to sit at a real table rather than this folding beauty we have here. And second, that's not really what I mean. The house is just a metaphor."

"Look, don't go all English teacher on me. You know I hate when you do that."

"And you know I hate seeing you like this. Joanna and I have been trying to get you to come out with us, do something—anything—but all you do is work and sleep. Have you even dated since Danielle? Have you even been laid? Why don't we get you a pet?"

Joanna and Molly have the kind of relationship Kat's dreamed of. They've been together for nearly ten years and are still as in love with each other as they were their first summer together.

"That's not fair. You know I travel nonstop and sleeping becomes a priority when I'm home. For the millionth time, I'm never home to take care of a pet. Plus, I'm too old to date and I don't do one-night stands."

"Kat, you're thirty-fucking-five. Last time I checked, that doesn't qualify you for social security benefits. You don't need to take so many games. You work way over your quota. I've known you too long to have you pull that bullshit on me. And maybe you need one one-night stand. You know, just clear the cobwebs out downstairs." Molly grabs her bag and walks to the front door. "I need to go. I have a cat that needs fluids in thirty minutes. Look, you know I love you. I just want you to be happy."

"I am happy," Kat responds, as if she's trying to convince herself of the fact as the door slams closed and the sound echoes around her in the empty house.

After Molly leaves, she sits alone at her folding table playing with her chopsticks for a while, trying to think of what she wants from life. The thing is, she could be okay like this. Life is easier this way. Fewer distractions, fewer issues to deal with. Why is living alone such a problem? It's not like she wants drama or to change her life completely. She doesn't need anyone. She is perfectly content with her own company. So okay, she misses—no longs for—the physical touch of another human being next to her, but those moments pass. Or, at the very least, she has learned how to ignore them completely.

"I am absolutely not going through a midlife crisis," she says aloud to the empty room as she drinks the rest of her beer.

An hour later, Kat lies in bed trying to fall asleep but all she can think of is the first time she and Danielle kissed outside Danielle's apartment. It was summer and the moon was full. Just remembering that moment and the way Danielle gently leaned against her gives her goose bumps. She pushes the memory to the farthest corner of her mind and wills herself to fall asleep.

Chapter Two

Danielle Jenkins made Kat stop in her tracks the first time she saw her walk into a room. Her wavy brown hair and light brown eyes combined with a nearly six-foot slender frame was certainly a showstopper. Kat recalled standing in a crowded cocktail party that Molly and Joanne dragged her to. The host was some college friend of Joanne's and had this ridiculously huge house in New Jersey overlooking the Hudson River and the New York City skyline. Kat felt out of place at such a high-end affair, although everyone was very interested in her work as a basketball official so conversation was easy.

While she chatted with a complete stranger about the state of US women's professional basketball in that crowded room filled with noise and laughter, Danielle walked through the door and all noise just fell away. Danielle looked down shyly as she entered the room and just like that, Kat was mesmerized.

She watched Danielle for most of the party without talking to her. She didn't mention anything to Molly or Joanne about her immediate attraction to Danielle since they were both loaded and sneaking off to make out, anyway. It's not that she was afraid of introducing herself to Danielle, but Kat felt like she was watching a piece of art move from room to room. She noticed the way Danielle tilted her head back when she laughed and the way her slender fingers gently gripped the stem of the wineglass. Most of all, she saw the easy way she had with people, friends and strangers alike.

Toward the end of the evening, Kat took advantage of a quick moment when Danielle stood alone on the patio overlooking the lights of New York City and the Hudson River.

"It's quite a view, isn't it?" asked Danielle as Kat approached.

"It sure is," Kat replied, not taking her eyes off of her.

Kat smiled, as did Danielle. "You've been watching me," said Danielle.

"Yes," Kat said. "Is that a problem?"

"Why did it take you so long to talk to me? I've been waiting all evening."

And so it began. They talked on that rooftop for over an hour, until most of the guests departed. Molly had to basically drag Kat away. The next day, the two met for a cup of coffee and ended up spending most of the day walking around the Village neighborhood of New York City and talking.

During those first two meetings and many more after that, Kat learned about Danielle's background in a noisy family of seven kids, which Kat just couldn't imagine since she was an only child. Their upbringings couldn't be more different. Danielle's parents were still married after thirty years. "They still have date night every Friday and sometimes, when I watch my father look at my mother, I know what true love looks like," said Danielle.

They continued to see each other and Kat learned about her love of horses and her ability to make absolutely everyone feel comfortable, including Kat. In Danielle, she saw pure goodness and light. It was the first time in her life she was around someone whose positive energy illuminated every corner of a room. Kat was drawn to her like a moth to a flame. They began dating immediately.

Kat soon found herself spending every free moment with Danielle in between travel and work. Danielle had a steady life as a forensic accountant in a large law firm. To Kat, her career choice didn't seem to fit her warm and engaging personality. But Danielle told Kat she enjoyed the predictability of her work. She had regular hours, a routine, and a healthy paycheck. Her steady career gave her time to take care of herself and the people around her whom she loved. In truth, Kat just couldn't find anything wrong with her except for the fact that Danielle knew absolutely nothing about the game of basketball and had no interest in sports whatsoever.

"I can't understand how someone who is nearly six feet tall was never asked to play basketball," Kat said incredulously one night after they had moved in together.

"I never said I wasn't asked to play basketball, volleyball, or just about any other sport. I wasn't interested. All of that running around, getting sweaty, I just don't see the point of it. I don't understand why you'd want to run up and down a basketball court for a living. To me, that makes no sense."

"And I can't understand how you could sit in an office staring at a computer for eight hours a day," responded Kat.

It used to infuriate Kat that Danielle could polish off a pizza, a six-pack of beer, and ice cream yet never work out and never gain an ounce. "Listen, I have a speedy metabolism—don't blame me."

"That's not speedy, it's turbocharged," was Kat's retort.

They began to spend more and more time with Molly and Joanne, becoming a close-knit pod of four. To Kat's surprise, Danielle and Joanne really hit it off, quickly forming a close friendship. This didn't bother Kat at all, in fact, she loved that Danielle and Joanne would hang out and do things together. Kat never truly warmed to Joanne, even though she saw how well she treated Molly. They just never seemed to connect and things always felt forced between them. But with Danielle and Joanne being close, it took the pressure off Kat to try to make a friendship where there would never be one.

After Kat and Danielle had been living together for several months, other seemingly innocuous things crept into the relationship little by little. Danielle never remembered to refill the ice tray. She'd leave wet marks on the bathroom rug. She didn't like that Kat traveled so much. Danielle pushed Kat to spend time with her family, but for Kat, this was like asking her to visit the gynecologist. She hated the loud, disorganized gatherings of Danielle's huge family. Where Danielle felt totally at home, Kat felt completely out of place. Time after time, Danielle asked Kat to talk to her about her background and her upbringing, and every time, Kat would tell her simply she was an only child and that both her parents died when she was young.

Even when they made love, Kat never felt reckless abandon or unrestrained passion. Danielle was solid and steady, but Kat never ever felt the "thunderbolt," which was a code word she and Molly had come up with when they were ten years old and thinking about what it would be like to fall in love one day.

"It will feel like we are hit by something gigantic," said Kat.

"It will feel like we are hit by a thunderbolt," mused Molly. And so it was etched in stone. From that point on, whenever Molly and Kat would talk about their new relationships the thunderbolt was the point by which all loves were weighed and measured.

"Did it feel like you were hit by a thunderbolt?" Molly asked one night when Kat talked to her about Danielle.

"I felt drawn to her warmth."

"That's not the same thing."

"Did you feel like you were hit by a thunderbolt when you met Joanne?"

"Yes. It nearly knocked me off my feet it was so intense."

"What if I never feel that for Danielle?" Kat asked.

"Then she isn't the one."

"But we fit together so well. What if it's just not in the cards for me to feel like that with someone? What we have could be enough."

Molly thought about this for a moment before responding. "Honey, we all can feel the thunderbolt, but sometimes we aren't willing to feel it. Those are two different things. One of these days, someone is going to open you up in a way you never knew was possible. She will know things about your soul that you never admitted to anyone. She won't just feel like home, she'll feel like you found the part of you that you left hidden long ago."

"But maybe I don't want all that exploration and personal growth. What's wrong with the life I have?" Kat asked.

"Nothing is wrong with the life you have. Only

you can know whether what you have is what you want."

"Maybe it's enough." Kat shrugged, as if trying to convince herself.

"Maybe it is, and maybe it isn't," Molly said. "Only time will tell."

"Oh, okay Buddha."

"Listen, I am no Buddha. I'm a Jedi Master."

Chapter Three

Kat is superstitious by nature. It's one of the by-products of growing up an athlete. Whenever she arrives in a hotel room, as she has just arrived in Seattle on this early August day, she unpacks her single bag as if she is moving in for good. It takes time and is completely inefficient given that she only stays in a room a night at a time. Nevertheless, she unpacks completely each and every time in order to make the room feel more like home and less like the sterile, impersonal space it really is. She places the childhood photo of Molly and her on the nightstand. In the past, when traveling, Kat placed a smiling photo of herself with Danielle when they went camping at Lake George the first summer they were together, but she threw the photo out in Sacramento—the first road trip after Danielle's break-up note. Once Kat is satisfied that the room looks like home, she heads to the gym for a quick workout before leaving for the arena.

On this particular road trip for a series of West Coast games well over halfway through the season, Kat makes her way down to the hotel gym where she spots Deb Henderson, a short, scrappy veteran official working tonight's game. Deb is known for her fairness, her even manner on the floor, and her incredible joy of life and sense of humor. She's also considered an absolute maniac in the weight room although she's nearly fifty years old. Kat has known Deb since her first game in the WNBA seven years ago. They've become pretty good friends over the years and surprisingly, they live only a few miles away from one another in New York.

"Hey, kiddo. I thought you missed your flight. You're usually here before me." Deb does chair dips with a twenty-five-pound weight in her lap, barely out of breath.

"Hey, Deb. I did miss my flight. I caught the second one out from LaGuardia instead of the first. Apparently, my ticket had me tagged for another search."

"Ugh, don't you hate that? I told Marty I was searched three times last month alone. I mean enough is enough."

Kat begins to stretch, although she hates to do it because it's yet another reminder that she's growing older.

"Hey, so how about you come out with us tonight? We're going to the Double Header after the game for some drinks and dancing." Deb is one of the only referees who knows that Kat is a lesbian, and Kat prefers it that way. Deb also knows about her troubles with Danielle and has been desperately trying to get Kat back on the horse again.

"Deb, you know I never go out to gay bars. I don't want to be around any of the other gay players or fans." Done warming up, Kat grabs two twenty-pound hand weights and begins to do a set of chest flies.

"Yeah, I know, Kat and her rules. When are you gonna live a little? It's not like it was a few years ago. There are gay players and straight players, gay officials and straight officials. Who cares?"

"I care," Kat replies as she finishes her first set.

"Well, if you change your mind, meet us there. I

have some friends coming in. It'll break up our boring routine a little."

"We'll see," Kat says as she starts set number two. "That's your special code for 'not a chance.'"

ฅฅฅฅ

During warm-ups, Kat stretches as the players prepare for battle. This is her favorite time: the calm before the storm. She loves how each pregame, night after night, has the same pattern and routine, although the pain of not being one of the players on the court has never subsided. Despite receiving a full-ride scholarship to Notre Dame, Kat never made a WNBA roster. After two years of disappointing WNBA tryouts, she decided that come hell or high water she would be on that floor. So she worked her way up the officiating ranks to become one of the game's premier female officials and only one of thirty WNBA officials. Yet, even after all these years, she still misses the team camaraderie and the joy of playing the game. While officiating is as close to the action as she can get, it's just not the same. Although she is a part of the game, she is not the primary focus of it. In fact, the better the referee is, the less you even notice her on the floor.

Kat's worked many games with this evening's crew: Deb the lead umpire, Jack on the clock, and Marcus on the floor with her. The music is ridiculously loud and it's nearly impossible to talk, so Kat takes in the above-average crowd and spends twenty minutes before the start of the game watching both teams warm up as she stretches. The Seattle Storm always puts on a great show for the fans, and the fans support their team one hundred percent. Seattle is one of the best markets for women's basketball next to Connecticut, but no one really knows why. It's not unusual to see Sue Bird or Lauren Jackson grace the cover of the sports section in Seattle, and Kat just loves to work games here because of that energy and the city's love and support for their team.

A new player from New York catches Kat's eye. She's relatively short at around five feet eight inches tall and explosive off the floor. This is the first time Kat's officiated a New York game all season, so it's the first look she's getting at the rookie everyone is talking about. Wow. She can shoot, Kat thinks. Kat hasn't seen elevation like that on a jump shot except for Deanna Nolan in Detroit. Number fifteen. Definitely a guard. Definitely beautiful. *Wait beautiful? What's wrong with me? This is a game, and I am here to work it.* She turns her attention to Seattle's bench, but before long, her eyes are back on number fifteen with her green eyes and incredibly long eyelashes. As Kat stretches, she tries not to stare, but it's no use.

"She's good."

"Huh?" Kat is thrown for a moment.

Deb smiles. "You're looking at number fifteen, right? Short blond hair? She's a rookie from Utah. Julie Stevens. Girl can play. She sat out the last two seasons rehabbing a knee injury. I worked the McDonald's All-America game before she blew out her knee and she put up big numbers." Deb pauses for a moment and leans over to Kat as she stretches her arms. "Cute too and gay from what I hear."

"Jesus, Deb, and where do you hear these things?" Kat pretends she's not interested, but she is intrigued.

"Same place I heard about you, kiddo." Deb slaps Kat on the back. "I think she's single, just in case you were wondering."

"Deb! You know we can't date players."

"I'm just saying. Who said anything about date? Loosen up a little, kiddo."

As the players complete their warm-ups, Kat works extra hard not to look in Julie Stevens's direction, but once or twice her eyes wander over to her. Before Kat has a chance to stop herself, her eyes take in Julie's strong legs, toned arms, short white blond hair, and those eyes. What color are they? Blue? Green? God, she is beautiful, Kat thinks as she feels a flip-flop in her stomach she hasn't experienced in a long, long time. Perhaps since the first time she met Danielle. Not even when she met Danielle. A beautiful girl who can shoot is a deadly combination. Kat looks up to see Julie glancing over at her. Julie smiles. To her dismay, Kat's stomach flips again, so she turns her back quickly on Julie. *Jesus, was she looking at me? Focus, for God's sake. You have a game to officiate!* Kat is horrified that a rookie player actually thought she was staring at her. Before she has a chance to beat herself up anymore, the buzzer sounds. Game time. She jogs to the sideline as the lights go out for introductions and the Seattle Storm pregame video begins to play.

Chapter Four

The Seattle Storm pounds the New York Liberty in the first half, to the crowd's absolute delight. The whistle blows too much and Kat feels like she is spending an excessive amount of time at the free-throw line. Even officials are annoyed by a poorly paced game. Kat hates blowing the whistle this much and feels like their calls are getting too nitpicky. The basketball-smart Seattle crowd agrees completely.

Kat, Marcus, and Deb meet during a television timeout in the second half to regroup.

"Look, guys, this is getting rough. I don't want any fights out there. I don't want any ticky-tack fouls. Call what you see. Let me handle both coaches," says Deb as she wipes sweat from her brow."

"Clery is going to blow a gasket if we don't call an offensive foul on Stevens," says Marcus, who is always trying to keep the peace.

"Marcus, you call it as you see it. From my position, I haven't seen anything so I haven't called it. Kat, have you?"

"Nope. Not from my position, I haven't. It's about the only thing I haven't seen tonight."

The buzzer sounds a second warning to the players. Kat is the inbounding referee on the sideline. As she puts the whistle back in her mouth and bounces the ball waiting for the players to take their positions, number fifteen, Julie Stevens trots over to the inbounding position.

"Hey there, I'm Julie. Nice to meet you, ref."

"Hi," is all Kat squeaks out before her whistle uncharacteristically falls out of her mouth and onto the floor. Julie quickly bends down and grabs Kat's whistle off the hardwood.

"I think you need this." She smiles again, peering at Kat through those incredibly long eyelashes. Kat grabs the whistle and quickly wipes it off. "Thanks. Get ready. Ball in!" She hands the ball to Julie. In a flash, Julie tosses the ball inbounds and becomes a blur, cutting off one screen and then another. Kat shifts her position up the sideline to get a better view of her zone. Within three passes, Julie is next to Kat again. She sets her feet, receives a pass, and drills a three from the right wing. Kat holds up both hands to signal three even though it wasn't close. Julie was a solid foot beyond the line. Kid can shoot, thinks Kat as she sprints up court.

As play continues, Kat finds it more difficult to officiate the game. Even if Julie is not in her zone, she finds herself seeking her out, catching glimpses of her as she moves with stealthy grace across the floor.

There are some players who are so visibly joyous on the court that it's contagious. Julie Stevens is one of those players. Streaky, lightning quick, and talent laden, Stevens is having a great game in her debut and is clearly relishing every moment. For the first time in a long time, Kat almost feels like a fan and is enjoying watching her, as much as she tries not to. It's too bad Stevens didn't play this game at home in New York. Crowd would've eaten her up, thinks Kat.

Moments after the lopsided Seattle win, Kat, Marcus, and Deb jog into the tunnel to their locker room. As usual, Deb likes to spend some time talking over the game and any missed calls. Her love for the game makes her an incredibly honest referee. The three talk through positioning and, of course, the play on the court. Deb takes some notes.

"Man, did you see the rookie nail those threes? I'm tellin' you, Deb, kid's got ice in her veins. She's gonna put up some big numbers if she keeps that knee healthy," Marcus says as he unlaces his sneakers. "Fifteen points on five for seven shooting from beyond the arc. Not shabby."

"Marcus, you say that about every rookie who has a good game." Deb laughs.

"True, but I never really mean it. Stevens is the real deal."

"Well, Stevens better learn how to play some defense. She basically held up a banner and cheered every time Bird blew past her," Kat cynically replies after she downs a half a bottle of water."

"Go easy, Kat. You know how tough it is for the rookies to get used to the speed and pace of the game. I don't think playing against Bird in a debut and holding her to seventeen points is a bad outing. Kid played well over thirty minutes and had just two turnovers."

Marcus grabs his bags and heads for the men's locker room. "Ladies, I will see you when I see you. Heading home for a nice rest."

"Later, Marcus. Nice job tonight. When are you on my crew again?" Deb asks.

"Next Tuesday for Detroit and Los Angeles."

"Get your gloves out for that one," Kat says as she prepares to head toward the shower. "It's gonna be a battle. Those two teams hate each other. I'm so glad I'm not on your crew that night Deb!" Kat means it. She hates working the Detroit versus Los Angeles games and has seen her share of fights between the two.

As the hot water pours down on her, Kat closes her eyes. She relives the moment Julie handed her the whistle after she dropped it. *Did her hand intentionally touch mine? What the fuck, Kat, are you in high school? Snap out of it.* For some infuriating reason, she can't get those blue-green eyes out of her mind.

From the other stall, Deb's gruff voice shakes her from her reverie. "Hey, kiddo, come out to the Double Header. Take a break tonight."

"Deb, why do you always call me kiddo?" Kat yells from her stall.

"Look, at my age, you think I remember your name?" Deb chuckles, clearly entertained by her own joke. Kat does too.

"We'll see. I'll meet you there."

"Yeah, okay. That's code for you're gonna blow me off again."

Deb's words sting her. "No, I mean it. I'll see you there. I want to stop back at the hotel first."

"Okay, kiddo," yells Deb, who immediately starts humming a song terribly out of tune.

❧❧❧❧

Back in her hotel room, Kat actually takes some time to put on a small amount of makeup, including some dark charcoal eyeliner to bring out her smoke-colored eyes. She brushes out her long, straight black hair, begins to put it up into her standard ponytail, but suddenly decides to keep it down. She takes more care in dressing than she has in a while, wearing a pair of faded jeans and a worn, light-blue button-down shirt. As she tucks it in, she wishes she had something else to wear, but this is life on the road with limited wardrobe options. She takes one final look in the mirror and thinks: not bad.

Twenty minutes later, Kat steps into the Double Play, one of the most perfect lesbian dive bars on the planet. Poorly lit, worn barstools and floors, a beat-up bar, and a small dance floor: it's ideal. She spots Deb right away or rather hears her gruff laughter immediately. The bar is crowded and it takes her a minute to reach Deb, who is genuinely pleased to see her.

"Well look what the cat dragged in! This must be a special occasion. Let me get you a drink pronto before you get all shy on me and run for the hills." Deb hands Kat a glass, pouring beer from a pitcher and Kat is immediately grateful for her friend. After the introduction to Deb's other friends, two of whom Kat met on previous road trips, the group finds a booth near the dance floor and orders another pitcher. Kat takes a deep swallow of cold beer and is actually happy to be out for the first time in a long time. She allows herself to relax and enjoy herself. She even allows Trisha, one of Deb's friends, to drag her onto the dance floor. After a couple of songs, Kat and Trisha walk back to their table and Kat bumps into someone.

"Oh, I'm sorry," she says as she continues on.

"Oh, it's okay, ref. Nice to see you out! Where is your whistle? You should put that thing on a string or something so you don't drop it."

Before Kat even turns, her stomach flips. Slowly, she turns to look at Julie Stevens, smiling broadly at her.

"Right. A lanyard. Funny. Nice game tonight, Julie. Um, if you'll excuse me, I'm just leaving."

"Thanks. I don't think we've formally met yet.

I'm Julie Stevens. You are?" Julie holds out her hand.

"Um, Kat. Kat Schaefer. Nice to meet you." Kat takes Julie's hand. Julie holds it a moment or two longer than she should.

"So, do you come here much when you're in town?" Julie asks, her eyes twinkling.

"She never comes out with us," Deb interrupts, slapping Julie on the back. "Hey, Julie, great debut game tonight. I look forward to calling more of your games. They're gonna love you in New York!"

Julie grins and Kat marvels at her full lips. "Thanks, Deb. It was so much fun tonight. I'm just so blessed to be playing in the WNBA, let alone in New York."

Julie and Deb continue to chat about the game while Kat sits down on an open barstool at the end of the bar. Although she's had several beers, she orders a shot of Jack Daniels to calm her nerves. Hands literally shaking, she tries to look around the bar for anything that will take her mind off of Julie's tanned arms. Julie leans over and whispers, "See anyone you like?"

Mortified, Kat quickly downs her shot and says nothing.

Julie laughs, entertained by Kat's discomfort. "Aw look, you're blushing."

Kat wriggles in her seat. "Look, I'd better be going. I have a long flight tomorrow."

"So do I. Dance with me before you leave."

Kat raises her eyes to look at Julie. Even in the dark, she can see Julie's blue-green eyes shimmer and she feels the butterflies in her stomach. "I really shouldn't."

"Why not?" asks Julie as she runs her long fingers through her short blond hair.

"Because you're a player and I am a ref, that's why."

"Well, look, I won't talk about work if you won't. Deal?"

Kat hesitates and rises as if to leave but Julie quickly takes her hand. *I Put a Spell On You*, sung by Jay Hawkins, begins to play.

"One dance," Julie says. "I love this song. Please."

Before Kat has a chance to respond, Julie pulls her onto the crowded dance floor. Kat places her hand on Julie's strong shoulder and feels Julie place her hand on the small of her back. Just that simple touch makes Kat's toes tingle. They begin to move slowly, politely, but after a few turns, Julie pulls Kat closer. They move more slowly now. At first, Kat hesitates to make eye contact with Julie, opting instead to keep her eyes downward. But after a few turns, Kat raises her eyes to see Julie looking intently at her.

"You're a good dancer," Julie whispers so close to Kat's ear she has to hold her breath for fear of making a noise.

It's like Kat can feel the walls she's created crumble at her feet. The little voice in her head is screaming for her to stop. She barely knows this woman and doesn't normally make it a habit of dancing with complete strangers, not to mention current players.

As they move slowly around the floor, Kat's legs start to wobble, and as if Julie can sense it, she pulls her so close that their hips touch. Kat sighs and leans into her. Her lips graze Julie's neck almost involuntarily, and she can smell her perfume. Before she can stop herself, her hand is on the back of Julie's neck, moving up into her hair. Julie runs her hand up Kat's back and down again. Kat's not sure if it's the music or the alcohol or both, but her body is burning up and her hands are beginning to move as if completely out of her control. Before she can stop herself, her thumb moves up Julie's neck to her jaw, then brushes against her lips. Julie takes her thumb quickly in her mouth and in an instant, Kat's lips are there, kissing Julie fully and without hesitation. If Julie is surprised, she doesn't show it. Instead, she returns Kat's passion with a kiss of her own. When Kat feels Julie's tongue in her mouth, a low moan escapes her. The two stop moving and share the most intense, powerful kiss Kat has ever experienced. The song ends and couples around them begin to break up and leave the floor. Kat and Julie stay in the middle of the dark dance floor, staring at one another for what seems like an eternity. Both look almost shell-shocked, as if the energy between them runs so deep that neither one can or wants to break free.

Julie takes her hand and leads her off the floor. "We need to get out of here. Now."

Kat knows she's not thinking clearly. In an instant, the situation becomes perfectly clear to her as her brain screams, *What the fuck am I doing?*

Abruptly, she pulls away from Julie, putting the familiar walls back up. "No, correction, I need to get out of here. This was a mistake. A big mistake. I'm not like this."

Julie is clearly hurt. "Not like what? Not like the sexiest woman and best kisser I've ever met?"

"This didn't happen. Just forget this happened," Kat says as she turns to rush out of the bar, leaving Julie perplexed and standing alone in the middle of the dance floor.

Chapter Five

Back in the safety of her small, dark hotel room, Kat paces back and forth. *What the hell was I thinking? I could lose my job over this.* She moves from one side of the room to the other, talking to herself, stopping, shaking her head. It's not like her to lose control of any situation, ever. Kat likes things in their own respective boxes. Work never touches personal life and vice versa.

"I am better off alone," she says aloud as if willing herself to believe it once more.

But for Kat, being alone is not a new turn of events. Growing up, she has one lasting memory of her father: his brown leather bag packed, his cowboy hat set firmly on his head, and his boots clicking as he closed the screen door and walked out of her life forever.

Her mom tried to be a decent mother but being maternal just wasn't in her genes.

"Darlin' Kat, your mama ain't the type of woman to mother anyone," she used to tell Kat as an excuse. Kat remembers sitting on the bathroom toilet watching her mother put on layer upon layer of brightly colored eye shadow as she prepared for another drunken night out. Her mother would take a swig out of a cheap bottle of whiskey as she dressed. It was the first time Kat ever learned the true meaning of "pregaming."

"For God's sake, don't go bouncing that basketball all hours of the night. I can't get no more complaints from the neighbors, you hear?"

But that night and many others, Kat played basketball hour after hour, alone in the dark. It was an escape from the loneliness of that Nebraska house. When she played basketball, the world could spin off its axis but Kat was in her own world, a bubble of safety and security so real she could forget about everything else. When she played, she wasn't a lonely little girl who missed her daddy. She wasn't scared of her mama's incoherent drunkenness. She wasn't too shy to talk to anyone. She was a basketball player, pure and simple. Kat quickly learned that in Nebraska, basketball players—male or female—were respected, revered even. For her, the basketball court would always be her home.

Kat rummages through her overnight bag and pulls out a worn and frayed note that she keeps tucked in the side pocket. Sitting alone on the bed, she reads the last line over and over again as if willing herself to believe it: "I hope you find happiness in all those empty hotel rooms."

Kat looks around the empty hotel room. She can hear the buzz of the air conditioning unit. She can hear the sound of someone in the next room flushing a toilet. She flops down on the bed and closes her eyes.

She dreams that the sun is shining brightly and the breeze through the open window blows the white sheer curtain from side to side. Kat knows exactly where she is. Paris. Spring. Morning. She is lying on her back naked with her head turned toward the open window. She opens her eyes and sees the Eiffel Tower in the distance. She is so unbelievably content in this moment she doesn't want it to end.

She closes her eyes and feels a hand gently run down the length of her back. This is the first time she has really let down her guard and allowed herself to feel anything with anyone. She's always been so careful, so aloof, but there is something about Danielle that is so steady to her, so comforting.

Slowly, she turns her head and opens her eyes. She sees Danielle lying beside her, smiling. Danielle pulls Kat closer and soon after, Kat is on top of her, reveling in the feel of full body contact. Danielle kisses her, saying, "Good morning. I love you."

Kat feels butterflies in her stomach. In the next moment, she is on the dance floor and a hand at the small of her back pulls her closer. She opens her eyes and sees Julie looking at her with those unmistakable blue-green eyes. *Those eyes are like the ocean.* And though she tries to stop herself from kissing Julie, she can't.

Suddenly, Kat sits up in the hotel room, waking from the dream. It takes her a moment to remember where she is. She hears the sound of a headboard banging up against the wall in the next room.

"Fantastic," she says aloud as she heads to the bathroom to take a cold shower.

Chapter Six

Three weeks after the Seattle game, Kat still can't get that slow dance with Julie out of her mind. She's back to her regular routine of fly in, officiate a game, then fly out. She intentionally leaves no time for socializing and little time to think about the white-hot connection she felt with Julie. Since that night at the bar, she's worked two other games with Deb. If Deb saw what transpired between Julie and Kat—and Kat is certain she did—she acknowledges nothing, for which Kat is extremely grateful. The last thing she wants is to try to explain things to Deb or anyone else for that matter. She continues to tell herself that it was her own singular error in judgment; she was just lonely and had one too many drinks. But in the solitude of a flight or in those moments before sleep, she recalls that kiss, the feel of Julie so close to her, and her sweet-smelling skin, and she is more and more at odds with herself.

While Kat tries not to think of the intense attraction, she is also not beyond understanding it. She knows full well that she has absolutely never before experienced a connection like this one. She tries to convince herself that there is nothing there—no attraction beyond the physical, but the more she pushes the intense feelings for Julie aside, the more she dreams of Julie's touch.

As much as she misses sharing a life with someone, she is determined not to make the same mistake twice.

She gave her heart to Danielle and Danielle walked away without the courtesy of a personal conversation or a phone call, without understanding that Kat's career as an official was her fleeting chance to be part of the game she loved so much. But Danielle never understood her love for the sport nor her willingness to sacrifice so much of what she loved to be near it.

On this lonely night on the road in late August, Kat talks on the phone with Molly while she lies on the bed in her hotel room. Molly is the only person she trusts with this or any other secret. Actually, come to think of it, Molly is really her only true friend. From the moment they met on the playground at ten years old, they have been inseparable best friends. Both were tomboys, although Molly played soccer, a fact Kat has never quite forgiven her for since basketball players and soccer players have this weird, unexplained rivalry and disdain for one another.

Kat doesn't usually call Molly this late in the evening when she's on the road, so it's probably pretty obvious something is up. After she skims over the meeting with Julie, Molly is silent on the other end of the phone.

"Molly, are you still there?"

"I'm here, babe. I'm just thinking. The way you make this all sound, it was just one night and not even a fling. You didn't even sleep with her, right?"

"No. I didn't sleep with her."

"Well here's the thing: I can't understand why you would spend so much time telling me something about a little kiss that you are trying to make me believe means so little," she says in her own gentle but firm way.

Kat is silent on the other end of the phone.

"Do you remember when we decided what it

would feel like to fall in love?"

They were in their favorite hangout: the tree house Molly's dad built in her backyard. In their private domain, no topic was off limits, and no one else was allowed in except the two of them.

"Yes. We decided after careful deliberation that when we met our soul mate we would know because it would feel like we were hit by a thunderbolt."

"That's right. And unless we felt the thunderbolt, that other person wasn't our soul mate."

"I know. I remember.

"Look, Kat, I appreciate that you take your work seriously and this poses a problem for your job if you pursue it, but what's wrong with getting to know her a little bit? What's wrong with seeing if it was really a thunderbolt or bad beer goggles? Maybe you shouldn't be so content. Sometimes the best experiences in life are the ones that make us the most uncomfortable."

After they hang up, Kat lies in bed thinking about her best friend's words. Honest and thoughtful, Molly's always had a way of putting life in perspective for Kat. She's helped her through years of watching her mother drown herself in a bottle, and she is forever telling her it's okay to listen to her feelings.

If Kat is going to be honest with herself, now is truly not the ideal time to have these feelings. She's flying home first thing in the morning to officiate a game in New York tomorrow night and will see Julie for the first time in nearly three weeks. From the sanctuary of her hotel room, she hatches a plan. She will be all business during the game, but she'll ask Julie out for dinner afterward. This way, she can sit down and talk to her and see if her own feelings are a one-time thing or something greater.

Chapter Seven

Officiating a game at Madison Square Garden is always special and today Kat is the one with some pregame jitters. Not all arenas are created equal. Madison Square Garden is a magical place where the history comes alive the moment you set foot on the floor. Kat's favorite part of working a game at the Garden is walking out of the tunnel and onto the court. No matter how many times she does it, it never gets old. As she walks down the corridor from the officials' locker room, she always looks at the large photos lining the walls, from Muhammad Ali to Willis Reed to Theresa Weatherspoon and then bam, she is out on the floor where so many magical sports moments transpired. The acoustics at the Garden are also different, and the raucous sound of the New York crowd always makes it seem as though the fans are literally on top of the court.

As Kat begins her own ritual warm-ups, she casually glances over and sees Julie take the floor. The crowd cheers. Just as Kat suspected, they've fallen in love with their rookie shooter. As usual, Julie looks confident and beautiful. She looks Kat's way and smiles broadly, winking. Kat turns away, blushing and continues her sprints along the sidelines. A moment later, Julie jogs past her, whispering, "You can't pull a disappearing act here, can you?" Kat tries to ignore her, turning her back on Julie as she jogs by.

On this Sunday in early September, Kat's crew

consists of Dave Moore, Brian Young, and Susie Abrams. She hasn't yet worked with Brian and doesn't really care for Dave, even though he is the crew chief. Susie is okay, although she is a little slow in covering the floor during fast breaks. Kat knows this is going to be a battle since both New York and Washington are tied for first place in the Eastern Conference. Both teams know one another extremely well and the past few meetings have been a little rough around the edges.

Although uncomfortable with Julie's presence, Kat is interested to see how she plays tonight. The rookie novelty is gone because most teams have seen Julie play at least once. She is going to have a very tough matchup in Alana Beard, who is having a solid season, averaging over fifteen points per game. Beard has been playing with a fire that hasn't really been visible since her days at Duke University. Kat will work hard not to be a fan tonight, but she can't wait to see how Julie responds to the challenge.

In the first three minutes of the game, Kat knows she is in for a long and difficult night. The best-officiated games are the ones where the flow of the game is not impeded by the referees. When the fans and players don't notice the refs, then Kat knows she is doing a good job with her crew. Tonight is not one of those nights. As expected, Crew Chief Dave Moore is blowing the whistle a lot. Twice in the first minute of play, Dave blows his whistle and makes a call from across the court focusing on her zone and not his own.

"Kat, get in the game. You're missing calls," says Dave quickly as they move up court."

"If I see a foul, I call it. I didn't see a foul there," says Kat with the whistle gripped between her teeth.

At the end of the first quarter, Washington leads

by six but neither team can get in a flow because eleven fouls have already been called. Even the crowd is groaning. Julie Stevens is held scoreless but the story of the first quarter is Chasity Melvin for Washington who has eight tough points in the paint. Both coaches are anxious, barking at any official within earshot. Kat is used to the bantering of coaches, but she knows with so much riding on tonight's game, the coaches are a little more vocal and aggressive than usual. She tries to cut both coaches some slack.

As the players head to their respective benches and the dance teams take the floor during the television timeout, Kat and the rest of the crew get instructions from Dave, although it's incredibly difficult to hear with the pounding music.

"I don't want to see any hand-checking out there. You see a hand-check you call it," says Dave.

"Don't you think we're blowing the whistle too much? Eleven fouls in one quarter is a lot. They can't get into the flow of the game," says Kat. Susie and Brian nod in agreement.

"Dave, I know you want to call a tight game, man, but we gotta let them play," chimes in Brian.

"If we let them play, we are going to see a fight," says Dave.

Susie replies, "If we keep blowing the whistle we're going to piss everyone off and have to T-up one of the coaches. Which is worse?"

When the second quarter begins, it's as if Julie Stevens has been shot out of a cannon. She is absolutely on fire, hitting three three-pointers quickly. The third three is in the right corner, just in front of Kat. The moment she releases the shot, she turns to Kat while the ball is still in the air and says "money." To keep from laughing out loud, she clenches down hard on her whistle. Julie winks and runs down the court.

Alana Beard tries to answer, but it's clear this night so far belongs to Julie Stevens. With the first half in the books, Julie Stevens struts off the court with five threes, scoring fifteen of her team's thirty-two points. Her team leads by four, 32–28.

As Kat walks into the tunnel at halftime, she hears Julie speaking with a television reporter. "It's not about how many points I score," Julie says, "I just want to do whatever I can to help my team win this game. This is our most important game of the season."

In the locker room, while Kat towels off and downs some Gatorade, the crew looks over first-half stats. "Stevens is hitting whatever shot she takes. Too bad for halftime. The Liberty could've ridden her all game long," Brian says.

It's not uncommon for a shooter to cool off considerably at halftime, so the odds that Stevens will come back lighting things up are slim. "Whaddya think, Kat?"

Kat thinks about Julie's smile as she said "money."

"Hello? Earth to Kat?" Brian nudges her with his elbow.

"Oh, right, sorry. I'm not sure Washington will let this one go without a fight."

Susie says, "It's getting chippy out there. I wouldn't be surprised if the bigs decide to push their weight around a little more in the second half."

Dave gives his final instructions as they head out of the tunnel and back onto the court. "Look, I know you guys thought I was calling things too close in the first quarter but I have a feeling about this game and I do not want it to get out of control. So, if you feel like you need to T someone up, do it and let's nip things in the bud."

※ ※ ※ ※ ※

The second half of the Washington Mystics against the New York Liberty at Madison Square Garden is a bloodbath. Players are fouling out left and right. Kat and the officiating crew are having a tough time keeping things in order. There have been elbows to the face, bloody noses, and several warnings to both coaches. Through it all, Julie weathers the physical play well, which is unusual for a rookie. While she's not nearly as hot as she was in the first half, she continues to score at a steady pace. It's a good thing too, because if it weren't for her, the Liberty would have lost their lead.

As the fourth quarter begins, New York is barely hanging onto a single-digit advantage. Julie leads all scorers with twenty-five points, but what impresses Kat the most is how she is keeping her cool. She looks like a Zen master playing basketball. While the battle rages around her, she moves almost effortlessly around the court and always seems to be in exactly the right place at the right time. Her teammates feed her the ball whenever they can and in this game, it's clear that a new team leader has emerged. Julie wants the pressure on her shoulders and she is rising to the occasion.

However, the Mystics refuse to go down easily and their attempts to shut down Julie have become more brazen as the fourth quarter winds down. But she is a rookie. She hasn't proven herself in this league yet so the officials, including Kat, let some contact against her go without calling a foul. It's up to Julie to perform; it's not up to the officials to hand her the game on a silver platter. She has to earn it.

Twice while Julie is shooting, potential fouls could be called and yet they aren't. Twice she misses. Both calls would have been Kat's to make. After the second miss, Julie glares at Kat and slaps her hand against her elbow, signaling to Kat she thought she was hit on the arm when she released the ball. "C'mon that was a foul. Blow your fucking whistle ref."

"Watch it number fifteen. One more of those and I will T you up. Take it down a notch. I only call what I see," says Kat in a serious warning tone.

"Then get a pair of glasses, ref," Julie snaps at her as they both run down the court.

Kat chooses to ignore the parting remark, but she is pissed off. That's the thing about being a ref. She can't do anything about that except move on and try to make the right call the next time down the floor. Julie is flustered and her emotions are now getting the better of her. She hits Alana Beard on the arm in a silly foul well beyond the three-point line. Kat blows the whistle and signals foul.

"Are you kidding me?" Julie stares at Kat hard. "You call that but you can't call it on the other end?"

Liberty Coach Moira Clery looks apoplectic on the sideline. Dave has to walk over to calm her down but all that conversation seems to be doing is making it worse.

Kat hands the ball to Alana Beard for each of the three free throws. Alana Beard calmly nails all three. The Washington Mystics take a one-point lead, 55–54 with just under three minutes left to play. Julie stares at Kat for the entire stoppage of play. Kat refuses to look in her direction, but she can feel Julie's stare boring holes into her.

After several uncharacteristically sloppy possessions by both teams, Clery calls a play for the Liberty for Julie to wrap around two stagger screens set for her in the post as she pops to the top of the key. She receives the ball on cue and uses her left arm to clear out Alana Beard, who has somehow stayed right with her. Julie rises and rises, higher and higher. She nails an unbelievably difficult three-pointer, but the shot is called off. Kat calls Julie Stevens for clearing out with her left arm, putting Washington into the one-and-one. Julie gets right in Kat's face and whispers, "Is this what you do to every girl you make out with on the dance floor?"

Before Kat can even really absorb the rancor in the comment, she blows her whistle and signals T for a technical foul. She calmly walks to the scorer's table and says, "Technical foul on number one-five, unsportsmanlike conduct."

Julie continues to complain. Kat glares at her. "I'm warning you, number fifteen, one more outburst and you are outta here. Cool down." Julie's teammates surround her and pull her away from Kat, trying to calm her down.

Alana Beard hits the two shots of the one-and-one. She hits the technical foul shot. On the out of bounds, the Liberty is caught sleeping and the Mystics get an easy layup. In the span of five seconds, there is a five-point swing in the game and the Mystics now lead 61–54 with under a minute to play.

The rest of the game is anticlimactic. The Liberty can't climb back. Julie has mentally checked out of the game and the Mystics shock the home crowd and steal first place in the Eastern Conference.

After the game, Kat takes some time in the locker room to write down her notes of the game. She always does this after a particularly difficult game in which technical fouls were called in case any of her work is questioned. Dave approaches her in the locker room and says, "I would have teed her up two possessions before when she ran her mouth off at you the first time, even though I have no idea what she said to you. She's still a rookie—she's got a lot to learn." With that, he grabs his bag and heads for the door. "Well, see you in a couple of weeks. I'm off to Houston tonight."

"See ya, Dave," Kat says. She finishes her notes and takes a long shower. The other officials have cleared out and she has the locker room to herself. So much for her big plans. There is no way Julie is going to want to have anything to do with her after tonight. The thought of going back to an empty house is almost too much for her to bear so she dawdles for as long as possible in the locker room. She checks her cell phone but has no messages and only junk emails to delete. Finally, after about an hour, she packs up her bag and heads for the door. She walks down the long corridor to the elevator and just as it's closing she yells, "Hey can you hold that?" She sees a hand stop the elevator and she rushes inside only to see Julie looking blankly at her. They are alone in the elevator. *Shit*, Kat thinks. *Shit. Shit. Shit.*

They stand in silence for a few moments. I'm not going to apologize, thinks Kat. I made the right call. She looks up at Julie who is staring straight ahead. As the doors open, Kat gently holds Julie back by the arm but says nothing. The two face one another. Kat looks at her, resisting the unbelievably strong urge to pull her close. Instead, she says, "I made the right call, Julie. You may not want to hear it, but I made the right call."

As she walks out of the Garden players' entrance, she's hit with the early September breeze and the sound of midtown New York traffic. She turns back for a moment but Julie is nowhere in sight.

Chapter Eight

On a rare afternoon off, Kat sits at the end of the bar in her neighborhood with a shot of Jack Daniels and a beer. She's in the middle of her own personal pity party and that's fine by her. After her meeting with Julie in the elevator, all thoughts of what could be between them are smashed. Kat took that interaction as a slap in the face to wake her up. Players and referees cannot be together. It's that simple. Two different worlds, two different lives, and that is that. But if it were so simple, Kat would turn off her feelings for Julie. The problem is, she just can't. She finds herself thinking of Julie constantly throughout the day. She wonders if she prefers the window seat to the aisle, wonders what her favorite meal is, wonders what it would feel like to spoon with her after a long day. She wonders what her naked body would feel like against her own.

If she could forget about Julie Stevens completely, she would do it in a second. Yet Kat knows that something happened in that bar when they danced. Her heart was stolen right out from under her and she is completely at a loss for how to get it back or make it stop.

And so she drinks another shot of Jack and closes her eyes. The music isn't helping. Any song by Adele only worsens her mood.

When Kat and Danielle were first together, the two were inseparable. Kat remembers how much they both loved to listen to music. They'd lie on the couch wrapped up in each other's arms listening to Vivaldi or Aerosmith and anything in between. In those moments, Kat thought she'd finally found a home. After all, her childhood wasn't exactly warm and fuzzy. She had no dad and no real mother to speak of. There were so many nights in Nebraska when she would lie with only her basketball and stuffed animals around her listening to Joan Jett or the Bee Gees or Whitney Houston and she wondered if she would always feel so alone. Being with Danielle showed her a different life. Being with Danielle showed her that someone could actually care for her in a way she always dreamed, and coming home to someone who loved her was all she wanted.

Somewhere along the way, things changed. Kat worked more, trying to keep up with Danielle's stronger earning power. Housing prices near New York City were high and it took both of their savings to afford the down payment. Even though Kat did well as an official for the WNBA and the Big East, Danielle was a forensic accountant for a big law firm. It was Danielle who made more money and Kat secretly felt uncomfortable with their lopsided earning power so she took every game she could squeeze in. Danielle began to resent Kat for her longer and longer hours on the road, even though Kat constantly told her she was doing it all for her, for them, and for the life she hoped they'd have together.

Danielle became more distant. They talked less, rarely made love, stopped listening to music and Kat began to see that the life she was working for was slipping away. When they finally bought the house, Kat hoped they'd turned the corner. They had fun furnishing the place. Kat would cook lavish Sunday dinners and invite their friends over to enjoy their home, their new life together. For Kat, everything was falling neatly into place. She had the house. She had the girl. She had a career in the game she loved so much. Then bam. The note that changed everything and she never saw it coming.

Sitting at the end of this near-empty neighborhood bar, Kat finally recognizes the problem. How could she have misjudged the situation so badly? The one thing Kat has always prided herself on is her ability to weigh and measure every decision. She is truly practical by nature and has never been the kind of person to hope and dream her life away. Kat's always trusted her instincts. She rarely trusts people, and her instincts are always solid. But how could her instincts have been so utterly wrong with Danielle? And worse yet, how could she ever trust herself again?

And so that brings Kat full circle back to that unbelievable kiss with Julie. Yes, she felt something. She felt it from the depth of her soul to the tips of her toes. But how can she trust it? There is no trusting herself anymore. The best she can do is fantasize a little and try to let it go.

"Do you want another drink?" asks the bartender.

"No thanks. I'm good, Mick." She resists the urge. Every time she thinks she's getting drunk, she thinks of her mother and pulls back. She throws some cash down on the bar and heads out the door, thinking about where she's headed next.

Chapter Nine

Jesus Christ, Katherine, I don't have an alcohol problem. What kind of stupid question is that?" Once again, Kat's mother is falling-down drunk. She knows better than to engage her mother in any meaningful conversation when she is loaded, but she is angry. At seventeen years old, she works as a waitress in the local diner to pay the bills since her mother can't hold down any job for more than a week or two at most. Every other waking moment between work and school, Kat plays basketball. Her coach wants her to play summer league, but she knows she can't—someone has to work so the electricity won't be shut off again.

"Please, Mama. You need to get a job. I can't do it all alone. You promised me you'd stop drinking," Kat pleads with her mother as she helps her undress.

Her mother yanks down the rolling vinyl window shade and crawls under the covers, even though it is seven in the morning.

"Baby doll, be a good girl and let your mama get some sleep."

"Mama, I have a big game tonight. Maybe you can make it to this one?"

"Sure, baby. Sure."

Kat stands in the doorway knowing her mother will sleep it off while she is at school. She also knows that instead of coming to her basketball game, her mother will be out drinking again by late afternoon. She closes the door to her mother's bedroom and slumps down at the kitchen table to eat her dry cereal without any milk.

The little house they rent is shabby, at best. The couch has holes in it, the kitchen chairs are rickety, and Kat never has enough money to pay all the bills and buy groceries too. Her food for the day consists of dry cereal and a peanut butter and jelly sandwich made out of the two ends of the bread. Hopefully, Mrs. O'Brien will feel bad and let Kat have some fruit or leftovers from lunch. Being best friends with the daughter of the cafeteria manager definitely has its perks.

At school, Kat is quiet, reserved. She is friendly to everyone and doesn't belong to any particular group except for the athletes, although everyone respects her for her prowess on the court.

"Hey, good luck today," yells Mike, one of the best players on the boys' team who everyone knows has a crush on Kat, although she is totally not interested.

"Knock 'em dead," yells Mr. Willis, the gym teacher who never fails to make one of her games."

Every school day passes the same way: she tries to concentrate on the Civil War or Edgar Allan Poe or algebra, but all she can do is tick down the minutes until she is on the basketball court. After all, this is her senior season, her shining moment to be captain and the true leader on the court. Nothing on earth is better than that.

At 3:15 p.m., she is dressed in her white uniform with gold-and-black trim and warming up. She is always the first one on the floor before a game. Kat loves the echo of her basketball bouncing alone on the hardwood floor. She shoots one after another, feeling the tension from her muscles fall away until there are no thoughts in her mind except for her movement and the connection to the basketball.

Today is a big game and Kat knows it. It's not because the game should be a close one, in fact, she knows her team should win. It's because her coach told her that college scouts will be at the game to watch her play. Some players would crumble under that kind of pressure, but she has been living with the pressure of being the primary breadwinner and caretaker for her mother for five years now. Playing basketball is a piece of cake compared to that.

In this game, Kat does not disappoint. She knows her performance in this game might well land her a free ride to a college scholarship. With each jumper, she tries not to think about the possibility of playing for Notre Dame basketball. With each drive to the hoop, she ignores the thoughts in her head about what will happen to her mother when she leaves.

She finishes the game with twenty-nine points, sixteen rebounds, five assists, and two steals. She has only one turnover. Her team wins easily by sixteen. After the game, her teammates get hugs from their parents who faithfully watch every game. The only one to greet Kat is Molly.

"Girl, you were unbelievable! Seriously. You know I know more about sewing than basketball, but I did what you asked and sat behind the scouts. They definitely liked what they saw."

"Great." But she doesn't seem that excited.

"What's wrong? asks Molly.

"Nothing, Molly. I'm just really tired. I've got to hurry up and get to work or Al will fire me for being late again. And, I'm so hungry!"

"I thought of that! Mom packed dinner for you."

Kat grabs the bag and looks into it, smiling. "Honestly, your mom is the best."

"I don't know about that. She gets annoyed with me for having a hair out of place but you two have some sort of lovefest going on. She told me to tell you that you can sleep over this weekend if you want to."

Molly's mom knows all about the difficulties Kat has at home with her mom and offers for her stay there every chance she can. Kat welcomes the idea of staying at Molly's—a home so unlike her own. Molly's house is filled with laughter and love. Hers is filled with silence and the stale smell of alcohol. She can never quite wrap her brain around how comfortable Molly's house is, but she knows a loving home when she sees it.

Finally, at midnight, after she works a full evening shift at the diner, Kat arrives home. She is beyond tired. She opens the door and tries to turn on the light but nothing happens. The power company must have shut them down again. Kat knows the drill. She uses the little flashlight on her key chain to find the matches in the kitchen drawer and she lights a few candles. She has homework to do but she's too tired to do it.

Kat throws herself down on her bed and falls asleep fully clothed. She feels like she is sleeping an eternity when she hears a muffled knocking at the door. She thinks she's dreaming so she turns over and pulls a pillow over her head. The knocking persists. After a few moments, Kat pulls herself up, rubbing the sleep from her eyes. The knocking continues. She grabs her flashlight and walks to the front door.

Groggy with sleep, she opens the front door to see two police officers standing in front of her. One of them she recognizes: it's Molly's dad.

"Hey, Kat, I'm really sorry to bother you. Can we come in for a second?"

"Um, sure, Mr. O'Brien. It's my mom again, isn't

it?"

The other officer tries to flick the lights on and realizes there is no power in the house. He takes his flashlight out of his hip holster and turns it on too.

"Sorry, the power, um, went out here again today. I guess I didn't pay the electric bill on time again."

"Kat, there is something we need to tell you. Your mom…"

Kat shrugs her shoulders. "Go ahead, Mr. O'Brien, you can tell me although this time I don't have the money to bail her out."

"That's just it, Kat, she didn't get arrested. Oh, Kat. I'm so sorry to be the one to tell you this. Hon, she was found dead outside the roadside bar."

Kat stumbles back. Officer Patrick O'Brien grabs Kat by the shoulders and pulls her to him. God knows she isn't his daughter, but she also knows he loves her like she is. "It doesn't look like any foul play. I think she just overdosed. I already went to the morgue so you don't have to do that, but we do have to talk in the morning about funeral arrangements."

Kat stares blindly at Molly's kind father. She used to dream he was her dad. Now it is official: she's an orphan.

Gently, and with such sadness in his voice, he says, "Look, Kat, go pack up your clothes and things. There is no reason for you to stay here anymore. You don't have to worry about paying the bills or getting the power back on. We'll make room at our place. You can bunk with Molly. Go, get your things."

She walks slowly back to her room and begins packing her suitcase. She takes down a few photos and posters from the walls. She folds her meager clothing and grabs her book bag. Before she leaves, she turns to look one more time at the sparse but clean room. God help her, but she is thankful to be leaving this place. The relief floods through her body so powerfully she forgets her mother is gone forever.

Chapter Ten

The remaining few weeks of the WNBA regular season are uneventful. Luckily, Kat is spared having to call another New York Liberty game, although she is compelled to follow Julie's progress throughout her rookie season. Her rise as an elite WNBA player is clear and she is not called out for any additional technical fouls. Then again, Kat hasn't had the opportunity to officiate any of Julie's remaining games, either. New York finishes their 2009 season only making it to the first round of the playoffs. Not surprising, they're knocked out by Washington. She works the Eastern Conference playoffs where the Indiana Fever beat the Washington Mystics handily. She isn't chosen to officiate the Finals between the Phoenix Mercury and Indiana Fever, which is a shame because Diana Taurasi puts in an incredible three-game performance to win the title. Angel McCoughtry of the Atlanta Dream edges out Julie Stevens for the 2009 Rookie of the Year Award.

Since their meeting in the elevator, Kat hasn't seen or heard from Julie. On several occasions, she wants to reach out to Deb to ask for Julie's number, but each time, she stops herself. She doesn't quite know how, but Deb always has every gay player's number saved in her cell phone.

In late September, Kat gets a call from the Big East about officiating conference games for the upcoming season as she has done for three seasons already, but she uncharacteristically turns them down. For the first time in a long time, she just wants some time off.

Instead, Kat looks around her empty house and no longer wants to see empty room upon empty room. Empty rooms equal empty lives, she thinks to herself, and she's tired of her own thoughts and feelings rattling around the whole house. So, to Molly's absolute joy she begins shopping. Kat shares the news with Molly over the phone.

"I can't believe it! We are going furniture shopping! Finally. Joanne, the eagle has landed."

"What the hell does that mean?" says Kat.

"Oh, it's just our secret code for when you finally decide to take charge of your life again."

With that, Kat puts herself wholeheartedly into Molly's capable hands. The two spend October driving miles upon miles to flea markets, antique shows, and furniture stores. Molly shops with a military discipline that scares Kat a little bit, but she is so grateful to have her friend's help with this daunting task that she willingly accepts it without complaint.

When Kat isn't shopping with Molly, she's painting. She chooses a color palette that reminds her of the beach. Yellows and blues and tans. Kat decides if she never returns to being a referee, she might become a painter. What could be better? When she paints, she can drown out the world with her music, Brandi Carlile in particular. She can sing as loudly as she wants, and she can drink beer as she works. With every stroke, progress is immediate and visible. The work is hard but rewarding beyond measure. As she completes each room, she feels the seven years of memories with Danielle being washed away or covered over. She tries to make each room a clean slate so she can finally call the place home again.

One afternoon, Molly and Kat walk through a gigantic outdoor flea market. It's a gorgeous bright and crisp fall day. Kat purchases a beautiful blue-and-yellow handmade quilt for the master bedroom. The old woman who sells the quilt informs her that the pattern is called Young Man's Fancy. "Don't worry," Molly says, winking at the old woman, "no young man is probably ever going to lay eyes on it again." Kat shoves Molly aside, laughing at her friend's innuendo.

As they make their way through the market, Kat purchases a few more items: an antique mirror, a great old trunk for a coffee table, and an amazing print called *Waiting in the Forest—Cheyenne* by photographer Edward Curtis. Molly thinks the print is depressing but Kat just loves that the man wrapped in the white cloth looks so out of place and in his element at the same time.

After they lug everything into Kat's house, they both plop down on the new couch and put their feet up on the new coffee table trunk at the same time. Kat clinks beer bottles with Molly and they sink into the new couch with a sense of accomplishment and exhaustion.

Molly looks around, pleased with the décor. "It's perfect, Kat, not too much and not too little. The colors you chose really make me feel like I'm at the beach. Your place actually looks like a home."

"I know. It feels like my home, which I guess is more important."

Molly rummages around in her giant bag and pulls out a box. "I almost forgot! Consider it a re-housewarming gift!"

"What's this? Kat asks. She unwraps the gift to reveal a beautiful framed photo of Molly and her as kids with Molly's parents smiling next to them.

"What would a home be without family photos?"

"Oh, Molly, I love it. It's perfect!" She places it on the coffee table.

"So now, what's next?" Molly asks.

"Next, I'm going to start cooking again. Friday night I'm having a barbecue here, so come hungry."

Molly glances at Kat from the corner of her eye. "Really? Wow, Kat, that's great. Although Joanne will be pissed because she just lost ten pounds."

The truth is, Kat used to cook all the time. When she wasn't traveling, she was in the kitchen trying new recipes and feeding all her friends. For Kat, there is something incredibly rewarding about making a special meal for the people in her life. She knows the urge to cook like that stems from her memories of staring into an empty refrigerator night after night when she was a child.

With her eyes closed, she can feel Molly's stare. "What do you want, woman?" She laughs, with her eyes still closed.

"You just haven't mentioned her in a while."

"What's there to mention? I think everything that was going to be said was said in that elevator."

"Jesus, Kat, you're such a damned pessimist."

"No, I'm really not."

"Yes, you really are." Molly yawns. "You never used to be like that. You never used to be the one who had no hope. It's not like you. You've worked so hard to put your life together after your mom and then She Who Shall Not Be Named, but still you don't think you deserve love. I just don't get it."

"Are you done?"

"Yes, I am done lecturing for the day," Molly says as she takes another deep swig of beer.

"Good. Look, I don't know what you want me to

say. I'm just getting myself back on track. I doubt Julie wants anything to do with me. It was just this fleeting thing—you know, the kind of thing that keeps you wondering, but the kind of thing that just isn't meant to be."

"Well, dammit, Kat, if you're still wondering after all these months, have you ever stopped to consider maybe there is something really there to wonder about?

"Of course I have, but we are obviously at very different places in our lives and maybe we just don't fit together. Molly, she's a lot younger than me. Hell, we have a twelve-year age difference. Don't you remember how clueless we both were twelve years ago? Did you even know how to give a woman a mind-blowing orgasm then, let alone know how to handle an actual relationship?"

"Speak for yourself, babe. And, oh right. Fit together. Hmm, let me see. On one hand you had Danielle, who while lovely, had no common interests with you. Lord knows she hated basketball," Molly says.

"Hated?"

"Uh, yeah, she only told me that like a million times."

"Then there is Julie, who granted you don't know well, but let's face it, she has the same intense love of basketball that you do, and she understands that part of you that no one else does. So what, she's younger. You're a baby cougar. Big fucking deal. Sounds like you and she have nothing in common. You're right, you're an idiot for even thinking of her."

"Your sarcasm is not lost on me."

"Good. Now toss me that throw blanket and let's watch a movie, and you know which one I want to watch."

"Don't you have to get home to, Joanne?"

"Nope. I'm all yours tonight, babe. Joanne is out with work friends and gave me a free pass. So let's go. Pop that puppy in, Leona!"

Kat pulls out her DVD of the movie *Beaches* and turns on the DVD player, knowing they both can, and probably will, recite every line to the movie.

❧❧❧❧

Later that night, after Molly has gone home, Kat lies in bed fully awake, staring at the clock. As soon as she closes her eyes, her thoughts turn to Julie as they do nearly every night before she falls asleep. The fantasy rarely changes. They slow dance. She can feel Julie's strong body against her own. She feels her knees go weak. She looks into those blue-green eyes and is carried away to somewhere she has never been but has always hoped to go. She imagines slowly taking off Julie's clothes, the softness of her skin, the sound Julie would make as she runs her tongue all over Kat's body. She imagines all of it, and then she opens her eyes and looks around the newly decorated room that feels remarkably like yet another freshly decorated hotel room.

Something has to give here. Kat's never been big on one-night stands, but maybe she needs one. Maybe she needs to lose herself in meaningless sex with someone else to forget about what could be possible with Julie.

Kat is a pretty self-aware individual. Having had to take care of herself for so long, she possesses the basic skills to psychoanalyze herself and understands that her heart is pulling her in one direction and her head is clearly pulling her in another. It's not as though she's all that familiar with Julie. For all she knows, the Julie that

Kat has created in her mind is probably very different from the real Julie…although Julie did kiss Kat in the way someone really should be kissed at least once in her life. She remembers reading somewhere that "the heart wants what the heart wants." Why on earth her heart wants Julie is just totally insane to her, but it's totally happening. Kat pushes thoughts of Julie from her mind and tries to dream instead of game-winning jumpers as time expires on the game clock.

Chapter Eleven

Kat moves around the kitchen with graceful efficiency much like she moves around a basketball court. It's an unseasonably warm Sunday afternoon in late October, perfect for sitting outside and enjoying the just-peaked fall foliage too. This is the first time she's having people over alone, without Danielle, and it's the first time in a long time she's doing all the cooking too. She realizes how much she's missed her kitchen and how much she loves seeing her refrigerator filled to the brim.

Jason Mraz plays loud on the stereo as Kat prepares a veritable feast of goodness—from baby back ribs to fresh tomato salad, corn on the cob, roasted potatoes, and scratch-made cornbread. She moves inside and outside, setting up the grill and fire pit, making sure she has enough serving dishes, and mapping out the exact timing for each food to go in and out of the oven. She knows she's overdone it. After all, there will only be five of them total, but this is her way of saying thank you to the people who are more like her family than her own family ever was.

Kat's military timing isn't a second off. The moment she puts away the final pan and lights a candle in the kitchen is the moment her doorbell rings. She opens her front door to see two smiling faces in front of her.

"Hello, Mr. and Mrs. O'Brien! I'm so glad you could

make it. It's been a while, I know. Please come on in."

When Molly and Kat both moved from Nebraska to New York, Molly's parents were soon to follow after Molly's dad retired from the police force and her mom retired from the school cafeteria. Before Kat came into their home, Molly was an only child since her mom miscarried three times before giving up on having more children. When Molly and Kat grew up and both moved to the busier New York area, Molly's parents came too, saying they wanted a change of pace from quiet Nebraska to enjoy all New York City had to offer.

"Oh hi, honey," gushes Mrs. O'Brien as she hugs Kat tightly. "We were so glad you called to invite us over. It's been too long."

"Yes, it definitely has. Mr. O'Brien, it's good to see you."

"You too Kat-a-lac," says Molly's dad as he wraps Kat in a bear hug.

"I haven't heard you call me that in a long, long time."

"I really have no idea why he thinks that's so cute. It still makes no sense to me," chimes in Mrs. O'Brien. "Are Molly and Joanne here yet?"

"Actually, they're right behind you."

Molly and Joanne hug Molly's parents. Kat is surprised at how warmly Joanne greets her. They've all shared a lot of memories over the years, but ever since the breakup with Danielle, Kat's sensed Joanne's loyalty lies with Danielle rather than with her. It's not terribly surprising given how close they were before. Kat knows Joanne and Danielle are still close friends and that must be as awkward for her as it is for Joanne.

"See, Joanne, I told you we weren't late!" Molly smacks Joanne on the arm.

"Please, everyone, come in. I have lots of food!" Kat motions to them.

After Molly shows Joanne and her parents around Kat's newly redecorated home to rave reviews, Kat gets everyone drinks and they settle outside on the back deck.

"Kat, whatever you are grilling smells like heaven on earth," says Molly's dad. Patrick O'Brien is a big, burly Irish guy who always seems to have a smile on his face. When Kat was young, she wondered how someone who seemed to genuinely love people the way he did could succeed as a police officer. But he did succeed. He was respected and loved in the community and also loved by Kat.

"Ribs, Mr. O. Baby back ribs."

"Dry rubbed?"

"Yep. Who do you think I learned the recipe from? I remember all your famous neighborhood block parties. No one else cared about any of the other food except for your ribs. I just hope I do your recipe justice. Speaking of which, I'd better take everything off before it burns!"

Kat works the grill and puts the finishing touches on her dishes while everyone relaxes outside. She was always surprised at how well Molly's parents accepted their sexual orientation and lifestyle with open arms. "We don't care who you are with so long as they treat you right and love you the way you deserve to be loved," Kat remembers Molly's mother saying when they both came out to Molly's parents at the same time.

She and Molly still laugh over one question Mr. O'Brien asked at the time: "Who made who gay?" After they explained that wasn't the way it worked, he shrugged it off saying, "I can't really say I get it, but I love my girls no matter what."

Even Kat and Molly were surprised that neither ever made a pass at the other back then. "We were always sisters," said Molly after they laughed about it one night.

Kat takes a moment to watch her family enjoy the warm late October day on her back deck. Her family. Molly's parents accepted her into their home without hesitation. They handled her mother's funeral and paid for it out of their own pockets. They dealt with the landlord and helped Kat clean up the house. They legally adopted her so she wouldn't go into DCF custody for the year before she turned eighteen. Molly's parents were her real parents, and Molly was as much her sister as she was her best friend. Kat marvels at how lucky she is to have them in her life and her heart overflows with love for all of them, even extending to Joanne.

After they are stuffed to the brim on Kat's mouthwatering meal, Joanne helps her clean up the kitchen while everyone relaxes around the fire pit.

"This was really nice of you to do, Kat," Joanne says as she dries the dishes.

"Thanks, Joanne. I feel like I'm finally back on my feet. It's been a while since I cooked an actual meal." Kat pauses for a moment, unsure whether she should continue. "Is she okay? I mean, I don't want to put you in the middle of anything, but I'd like to just know that she is happy."

Joanne looks at Kat as if trying to decide how much information to give her. "She's doing really well. She's married, actually. To a corporate lawyer named Dawn. They've moved out to Colorado and are in the process of adopting twin boys."

Kat feels the earth shift a little under her feet so she leans against the counter for support. *Married?*

Colorado? Kids? So fast?

She tries to pull herself together enough to steady her voice. Molly didn't tell her any of this. "Really? Wow. That's great. I'm happy for her," she says a little too quickly to be believable. Her hand shakes as she puts a glass in the dishwasher.

Molly walks in, and Kat knows her friend will notice how thrown off she is at the news.

"You told her," she says evenly to Joanne. Her lips form a thin line.

"Yeah, babe. I told her," Joanne says with a shrug.

"No, you're right, Joanne. I did ask," Kat says. "And I'm glad you told me. It's fine. Molly, you could have told me. Really, I'm fine. Excuse me one second."

She rushes off to the guest bathroom and locks the door behind her. Splashing water on her face to pull herself together, Kat's not quite sure why the news of Danielle hits her the way it does, but it feels as though she's been knocked off balance. *I can't believe she is married. I can't believe she found someone new so fast. I can't believe she moved to Colorado and is adopting kids. Twin boys.* When they were together they never discussed kids. Yet only eighteen short months after their breakup, it seems like Danielle easily tossed away seven years with Kat for a new wife and a new life. And here Kat's been thinking she's got it together because she just cooked her first dinner in a home that finally has an actual kitchen table again.

Molly's mom gently knocks on the bathroom door. "Hon, you okay?"

Kat opens the bathroom door, her voice shaky. "Yeah, I'm okay."

"So you heard the news about Danielle, I presume?"

"I did."

"Oh, honey. Come here."

Mrs. O'Brien wraps Kat in the perfect motherly hug and Kat just melts into it. Molly's mom is the mom she never had, and she treasures moments like this when she can feel the love wrapping her up. This was the hug she always yearned for from her own mother that never came. This was the hug Kat remembers getting at the cemetery after they buried her mother. This was the hug that makes even the worst news seem bearable.

"It's okay, honey. Everyone goes through life at her own pace. You and Danielle just weren't meant to be. But that doesn't mean something wonderful isn't around the next corner waiting for you. You know what they say—"

Kat interrupts. "When God closes a door, a window opens."

"Right. Now let's get a slice of that apple pie I made."

"With ice cream," says Kat.

"Definitely."

Chapter Twelve

Two weeks later, Kat is swearing at herself in the car for accepting Deb's fiftieth birthday party invitation. Although Deb's house is just a thirty-minute ride into New Jersey from Kat's, she isn't in the mood to hang around a bunch of officials talking about basketball. Since the WNBA season ended, she hasn't watched basketball, hasn't picked up a ball to shoot around, nothing. It's as if she's wiped basketball off her map completely and to be honest, she's enjoying the clean break.

Kat stares at the front of Deb's neat little raised ranch. It's a cool, clear, late fall Sunday afternoon and, unsurprisingly, cars are parked around the block. Deb loves a party and knows plenty of people who love to party too. Kat walks through the front door and up the stairs to the living room feeling rather uncomfortable. After scanning the room, she's surprised she doesn't recognize a single face. Just as she turns to make a run for it, she hears that unmistakable voice from the kitchen.

"Kiddo, you get your ass in here and wish me a happy birthday!"

There's nothing she can do now. She's stuck. Immediately, she begins thinking of what excuse she can give to blow the party. *Stomach virus? Bad guacamole? Viral infection? My cat died? Right, Deb knows I don't have a cat. Dammit.*

Kat walks into the crowded kitchen and sees a few people she does know. Deb slaps her hard on the back and Kat gives her a kiss on the cheek. "Happy Birthday, Deb. You sure know how to celebrate."

"Well Jesus, kiddo, I'm fifty, not dead! Okay everybody, who wants a shot?"

As usual, Deb is the life of the party. Kat doesn't have a chance to say no before a pink plastic shot glass is passed to her. One of Deb's friends cranks up the music and Kat has to laugh. So typical. Deb loves Madonna. After four quick shots and a bunch of laughing toasts, Kat excuses herself to get some air while everyone starts dancing around to "Material Girl." The sliders to the back porch are wide open so Kat moves out to the back patio to get away from the shot drinking and sees Susie, one of her fellow officials.

"Hey, Susie. How's it going?"

"Hey, Kat. It's good. I was asked to cover NCAA this year. I had to beg for the weekend off so I could come to the party. You reffing? I haven't seen you around."

"No, I decided to take the winter off. I needed a break," says Kat.

"I hear you. I wish I could but we need the money. Jack got laid off at the construction site so we just have my income. At least, he's able to stay home with the kids. Saves quite a bit on day care."

"Sorry to hear that, Susie."

The shots begin to take effect and Kat tries to decide how she can return to her car without going through the rest of the house. Realizing she's trapped in the yard, she turns to head back inside when she hears it. That voice. *Her* voice. Kat panics. Of course, Deb would invite Julie without telling her. Perfect.

Kat looks up to see Julie's blue-green eyes smiling back at her. "You weren't trying to make an escape were you?"

"Actually, I was. I've really got to go." Kat is self-conscious. All she can smell is Julie's perfume and she's convinced everyone at the party is staring at them.

Deb breezes through and hands Julie and Kat yet another shot in a plastic cup. "Drink up, kiddos!" She gives Kat a knowing wink as if to say, of course I saw you two at the bar and of course I invited you here to see her. Julie clinks Kat's plastic cup before downing her shot. She hasn't taken her eyes off Kat yet.

Kat puts her empty cup down and sways a little before saying, "Look I really should be going."

"Oh no, you're not going to drive. Let's go for a walk instead."

"It's nothing. I just haven't eaten much today."

She feels Julie take her hand and pull her deftly through the crowded party. In a matter of moments, they are in front of Deb's house in the relative quiet of her suburban neighborhood.

"So, which way?"

"Huh?" Kat is totally off balance and it's showing. Not a good look. *Pull yourself together.*

Julie senses her discomfort and laughs. "Which direction would you like to walk?"

"Oh, that way, I guess." She points left. She has no idea where that leads.

For a few minutes, neither of them says a word. They just walk in this weird silence. They turn a corner to the block and see an empty but well-kept playground. Julie crosses the road and walks over to the swings. "I always loved swings," she says, sitting down.

"You want me to give you a push?"

"Ha, no, I think I can handle it." Both sit on the children's swings and rock back and forth. After a few moments, it's Julie who breaks the silence.

"So, are we ever gonna talk about what happened?"

"Which time?" Kat says.

"Well, both I guess."

"Look, I don't want to get all into any drama. Really, I don't. I think you are a beautiful woman and an amazing basketball player but..."

"But what?"

"But that's it. Nothing. Let's just leave it alone."

Julie shakes her head. "That's it? You've decided this all on your own and that's it? Jesus, Kat, someone must have broken your heart into a million pieces for you to put this many walls up this fast."

"You don't know anything about me or my walls," Kat says defensively. The effects of the shots are disconcerting. She's losing control of something deep inside of her and it's quickly rising to the surface.

Julie stops swinging and looks hard at Kat. "Then tell me. I want to know."

Kat looks around the playground for any distraction she can find. *Where are the fucking kids? It's a Sunday. Kids should be out playing. Jesus, this playground is quiet.*

"Kat, please. I am here. I didn't come to this party to see Deb. I came here to see you. Let's get something straight. That kiss—that kiss was well, it was epic. I know I behaved badly during the Washington game and you were right to call that technical. I'm not mad about that. I was really angry with myself for letting you get under my skin. I've tried like hell to focus on basketball but truthfully, you are all I think about. You and that kiss and how I want to do it again and again."

Kat stands, trying not to make eye contact with Julie because she knows if she does, it'll all be over. "This can't happen. It just can't. You don't want any part of me. I'm not the perfect person you think I am."

"Who said you were perfect?" says Julie, standing in front of Kat. "I never said you were perfect. I never said I knew where any of this would go, either. All I know is that I want to try. Is that so bad?"

"You are twenty-three years old. What do you know about any of this?"

She turns to walk away but Julie grabs her hand. Before Kat can speak, Julie pulls her close—as close as they were when they danced. She lifts her chin with her finger. "There is no mistaking this. I know that for certain."

Julie kisses her softly at first, but the kiss quickly turns fierce with both Kat and Julie pulling one another closer. Kat breaks away first. Breathless, all she can manage is "Please."

Julie's eyes look like the deep end of the ocean. "You're not walking away from me this time."

Kat isn't quite sure how they get back to her house. The thirty-minute ride home is a blur. Thank God for navigation systems because Julie drives her home without difficulty and without asking for directions. All she remembers is opening the front door and seeing Julie walk in.

Before the door even slams closed, Kat is kissing Julie again. Deeper and deeper. They stumble up the stairs to the bedroom. Julie pushes Kat down on the bed and stops. She looks at her with an expression she can't quite place. There is so much certainty in Julie's eyes. Kat sits up and watches Julie slowly unbutton her own shirt. She drops it to the floor and begins unbuckling her belt, followed by her jeans. Slowly. Kat watches her and all the while is torn—should she look into those eyes or at that body?

Julie undresses completely. When she is naked, she straddles Kat and looks into her eyes before kissing her in a way Kat knows for absolute certain she has never been kissed before. It's as if she is drowning and being saved at the same time. Kat pulls Julie closer to her so she can feel her soft skin. She can't get close enough to her. Julie begins rocking gently and Kat matches her rhythm even though she is still fully clothed. Julie leans back. Kat kisses her neck, her throat. She licks her nipples and feels Julie's body respond. Kat rolls her over, straddling her. She removes her own shirt and bra quickly as Julie pulls at the buckle of her jeans. Kat can't get her clothes off fast enough. She just wants to feel every inch of her skin on Julie's. She kicks off her jeans and panties and in seconds, they are totally naked and entangled, touching, feeling, and kissing.

Their lovemaking is like nothing Kat has ever experienced. She's been with her fair share of women but no one has ever known her this instinctively. What Julie is doing to her might well be her undoing. She clings to the headboard. Flashes of light pass before her eyes and at one point it feels as though she's actually leaving her own body behind.

Turning Julie over, Kat works her way down her body. Julie arches her back just to make contact with her. Kat takes her time kissing her stomach, her hips, and her thighs. "Kat please," is all Julie can say, nearly writhing. Before Julie can take another breath, Kat's tongue begins an absolute assault on her clitoris. Flicking, rubbing, tasting her, her tongue plunges deep inside of Julie and then comes back for more. She sucks and rubs and tastes Julie until it's Julie who can't hold back another second. Kat tastes Julie come in her mouth and she swears it tastes like honey. But before Julie can relax, Kat's fingers are deep inside of her; her rhythm is slow at first, measured. Julie moans and begins rocking into Kat's hand, urging her, pulling her deeper and deeper. Julie claws at Kat's shoulders, dragging her up so they are face-to-face. Still deep inside her, their rhythm quickens and Kat feels ready to explode. Julie's eyes stay focused on Kat's. Neither blinks. Neither looks away. They climax together and Kat falls on top of Julie whose body involuntarily quivers over and over again.

As they make love, they do so in a combination of fast and slow motion, each taking turns pleasing the other. Just when Kat thinks they can't possibly continue, one touch lights another fire and so they begin again.

After hours of lovemaking, Kat is utterly exhausted. She and Julie lie side by side in bed, covered in sweat.

"Thirsty," is all Julie can manage.

Kat stands and takes a moment to regain her balance. She is actually wobbly. She makes her way slowly to the kitchen for water. Realizing she is starving, she decides to make something. In a matter of minutes, she whips up a spinach omelet, fresh fruit, and orange juice.

When she returns to the bedroom, Julie is lying in the exact same position she left her. Kat laughs.

"What is this?" Julie says.

"Breakfast."

"But it's three in the morning."

"So what. I love breakfast in bed."

Julie drags herself up to a sitting position and leans back against the headboard. Kat hands her a glass of orange juice and Julie downs it in seconds.

"Better," Julie says.

The two dig into the omelet and fruit and inhale all of it quickly, with no conversation in between bites.

"I'm not sure if I can stand up." Julie groans.

"Yeah, that was pretty tough for me too."

"Kat?"

"Um hmm?"

"That was..."

"I know," Kat says, interrupting her.

"No, I need to say this." She pauses before continuing. "That was like nothing else. When can we do it again?"

Kat laughs. "Give me a few minutes."

Chapter Thirteen

Kat wakes up to the sound of Molly's voice on the answering machine.

"Kat? Where the hell are you? I haven't heard from you in days. Are you alive? If I don't hear back from you in two hours, I am sending out a search party."

She has no idea what time it is. Judging from the sunlight, it has to be afternoon. She turns her head to see Julie's body sprawled out next to her. Julie lies on her stomach and the white sheet is barely covering a leg and a hip. Looking at Julie, Kat feels a rush of emotion that nearly brings tears to her eyes. They have been holed up in bed for three days. Three days of the most incredible lovemaking of her life. Three days of sheer bliss.

Julie yawns and stretches. She opens her eyes and sees Kat staring at her. Julie brushes a strand of her long black hair away from her eyes. "Good morning, sunshine," she says.

"Good morning," replies Kat. Julie slides over so that her head is resting on her stomach.

"Have I told you that mornings are my favorite time of day to make love?" Julie begins kissing her stomach.

"That's nice, but it's no longer morning. I've completely lost track of time."

Julie looks up, surprised. "Have I told you afternoons are my favorite time of day to make love?"

Kat smiles. "I think we need to move around, you

know, return to the land of the living."

Julie snuggles into Kat. "I guess you're right."

After they attempt a shower in between making love, Julie is dressed and upright in a pair of Kat's sweats and a tank top. She casually walks through the house looking around.

"Your house is really nice. But do you mind me asking why I don't see any pictures of your family?"

Kat sits down on the couch with a cup of coffee. "It's a long story."

"I've got time."

"I don't feel like going into it right now. Let's leave that for another time."

"Okay, then let's start with something simple. What is Kat short for?"

"Katherine."

"What's your middle name?" Julie asks innocently.

"Elizabeth."

"Now we are getting somewhere." Julie continues to move around the room.

"When is your birthday, and how old are you?" she asks mischievously.

"September nineteenth and I'm thirty-five," Kat says.

"Favorite color?"

"Hmm. Blue. Your turn."

"Well, my birthday is February twenty-sixth," Julie says. "I'm twenty-three. I know, don't roll your eyes. Yellow is probably my favorite color, although it changes depending on what mood I'm in."

Julie picks up a photo of Kat wearing a Notre Dame basketball uniform. "I didn't know you played ball." Her eyes are wide with surprise.

"Yes. I played ball." Uncomfortable with the

attention, Kat fluffs a throw pillow. "I got a full ride to Notre Dame but I didn't get that much time. I mostly rode the bench. Not like you, big superstar at the University of Connecticut."

"You know UConn and Notre Dame have an incredible rivalry, one I think UConn owns." Julie winks.

"I am so not going there with you."

Julie turns serious. "So what else?"

"Huh?"

"So what else do I need to know about you?"

"I'm not sure what you're asking."

"Are you with someone?" Julie asks.

"No. I used to be but it didn't work out."

"Why not?"

"Because apparently I am obsessed with my work."

"Ahh," says Julie. "Now we are getting somewhere. Actually, Deb told me a little bit about your last girlfriend. She said she was pretty but she had a stick up her ass about basketball. Something about her being a boring accountant."

"Deb told you all that, did she? Well, yes, Danielle is an accountant. I don't really think she has a stick up her ass, but I guess that's one way of looking at it. She is a good person. We were together for seven years before things changed. I'm not quite sure how it all went so wrong so fast."

Kat stands up and walks to the window. She stares outside for a moment. The phone rings. After the third ring, the machine picks up. Kat hears Molly's voice. "Shit. I've got to take this. She will call the police if I don't tell her I'm okay."

"Who is it?"

"Molly. My best friend."

"The other girl in your pictures?"

"Yes, that's her." Kat answers the phone. "Molly, I'm here."

"Jesus H. Christ, where have you been? I've been calling you for like three days!"

"I've been busy."

"Doing what? Oh, wait! I mean who? Or is it whom? I never get that right. Is she there? How good is the sex? Tell me everything!"

"I can't right now," Kat says, "but let's try to talk later, okay?"

"Kat, wait. Don't you hang up on me before giving me details, woman," Molly says.

With a click, Kat hangs up the phone.

"Hey, I've got an idea," Julie says. "Why don't we shoot around a little? Is there an indoor court in the area?"

"Do you think that's a good idea?" Kat says.

"Why not? You think we'll be too competitive with each other?"

"Um, yeah, it's just a guess."

"Okay. Ground rules. No games, no contests, no one-on-one, just simple and friendly shooting around."

Fifteen minutes later, Kat and Julie are lacing up their sneakers courtside at the local YMCA. The court is empty since it's a Wednesday and the kids are still in school, so they begin shooting around casually.

"Make it, take it?" Julie asks.

"Sure."

Kat is rusty and she knows it. She referees; she doesn't play. She can't remember the last time she enjoyed shooting around with the exception of a rushed shot in a pregame here and there. Kat takes a couple of shots in the paint and slowly works her way out to just behind the free-throw line. Julie watches her with the practiced eye of a professional sizing up someone to see what kind of talent they have just by watching a few jumpers.

"Well, I can see why you got a scholarship to Notre Dame."

"And why I was named Nebraska Player of the Year?" Kat misses a three. Julie snatches the rebound and starts shooting. Kat rebounds make after make.

"No way, were you really? How many points did you score in high school?" Julie asks, shooting jumper after jumper.

"Oh, that's not important," Kat says as Julie knocks down another jumper. "You gonna miss one anytime soon?"

"I'm not competing, I'm just curious. How many?"

"Two thousand one hundred and seventy-nine."

"No freaking way!" Julie stops for a second and holds the ball on her hip. She is clearly impressed. "That's more than me." Julie tosses the ball back to Kat who takes a jumper on the left wing and hits it. Julie rebounds the ball and passes it back to her.

"Yes, I know," Kat says. "I scouted you, so to speak." Kat shoots and misses, gathering the rebound and tossing the ball back to Julie.

Julie comes closer to Kat and gently pulls at the hem of Kat's tank top. "You did, did you?"

"Of course I did. But my high school scoring records were done out of fear or something else. It didn't translate as well once I got to Notre Dame. I just lost the fire, I guess, so I saw less and less playing time until riding the bench was my reality. You could say I was a big disappointment for a full-ride player. I mean I didn't win three National Championships like you did. I wasn't a First-Team All-American or anything like that."

"Wait. You said so much there I want to talk about."

"Why? It's ancient history," Kat says, shrugging it off.

Julie's hit a nerve with Kat. "Can we sit down for a few?" She motions to the bench. "So why did you say you played out of fear? What does that mean?" Julie places her full attention on Kat, making her feel self-conscious.

"Well"—Kat stops, trying to find the right words—"let's just say I had a rough time in high school family-wise."

"Tell me."

"Not now. I just can't get into all of it right now. What about you? Tell me what it was like to win your first National Championship or be drafted into the WNBA in the first round. How hard was it to return after your knee injury?

"Why do you do that? Downplay your own experiences or talent or past? It's weird. You should be so proud of what you've accomplished in basketball. Not many players can say they've even come close to what you've done."

"Listen, I don't want to get into a big discussion about my rotten childhood and the pain of not playing in college." Kat stands, hopefully ending the conversation.

"And there go the walls again," Julie says, shaking her head.

"What walls?"

"Oh, please, you're going to pretend like you aren't aware of what you are doing right now? Look, Kat, I think you are spectacular. Obviously, you can play. Don't push me away when I'm trying to get to know you outside of the bedroom."

"Maybe I'm afraid you won't like what you see and you'll just walk away."

Julie rests her hand gently on Kat's leg, looks at her with those endless blue-green eyes, and says just loud enough for Kat to hear, "I'm not going anywhere."

"I've heard that once before," Kat says.

"Maybe. But not from me you haven't."

Kat needs some breathing room. She snatches the ball from Julie's lap and drives the length of the court for a leftie layup. She continues to shoot around alone at the far basket for a few minutes until Julie walks over to join her.

Kat casually passes the ball to Julie on the right wing. Julie surprises her by taking a jumper almost at the hash mark. She hits the shot: nothing but net. The two continue to shoot, taking turns back and forth for almost ten minutes without saying a word. Kat sees how easily Julie can focus on the ball, on her shot, on the rim. There was a time when Kat could do the same thing.

As she watches Julie shoot jumper after jumper, Kat is completely mesmerized. Julie's shooting motion is so smooth, so seamless, it's truly a perfect jump shot hitting nothing but the net every time. And her vertical leap just blows Kat away. She would not want to guard Julie in a game scenario. Not at all.

After both of them work up a little sweat, Kat takes a rebound and hangs onto it. "You hungry?"

"I could eat, yeah."

"Let's go. I know a great place."

"Sure," says Julie.

Chapter Fourteen

A few minutes later, Julie and Kat sit in a casual, busy restaurant for lunch. Kat is oddly preoccupied with her menu.

"How long does it take you to pick out a sandwich?" Julie nudges Kat's foot with hers.

"Hmm? What? Oh well, I'm not sure if I want a salad."

"Ahh. Well, hopefully, that decision won't take twenty minutes."

The waitress stands at the table, waiting, snapping her gum. "Ma'am? Can I take your order?"

Kat looks up, flustered. "Um, sure. I'll have the turkey panini, please. Salad instead of fries. Oh, and an iced tea, unsweetened."

"Same for me," Julie says.

After the waitress leaves, Kat can feel Julie staring at her. She knows Julie senses her discomfort. She also knows Julie doesn't understand it. How could she? Although they've spent an incredibly passionate few days together, the fact remains that they still hardly know one another. A few days of great sex does not a relationship make. Kat can feel herself cooling off as reality sets in once again.

After an interminably awkward silence, Julie asks, "So, what's your plan for the winter?"

The waitress puts their iced teas down on the table.

"Thanks," Kat says. "I guess I have to earn a living somehow. I've taken about as much time off as I can before getting too rusty. What are your plans? Will you be playing overseas?

"Maybe. I might play for Milano in the Italian Euroleague. It's good money and really hard to turn down but..."

"What but? That's great. Everyone thinks WNBA players moonlight in the European Leagues but unfortunately, it's the other way around. The Euroleagues are where the real money is."

"Yeah, they will pay me triple my WNBA salary for a half season. I haven't told them yes yet," Julie says.

"Why not?"

"Well, I've been a little busy."

"That's sweet but stupid. You should go. You won't be able to play forever and you need to make the most of your time now. I wish I had that opportunity." Kat stabs at the lemon in her glass with the straw.

"So, that's it? I should just go and not even discuss this with you? Is that what you're saying?" Kat can see the blood pulsing in Julie's neck, but she can feel herself detaching just the same.

"Julie, we have very different lives. It's crazy to think the last few days have been more than just a..."

"A what? Go ahead and say it. A fling?"

Kat is silent. The waitress delivers their food. She must sense the awkwardness between the two because she disappears immediately.

"Is that what you think this is? Just a fling? Like I just wanted to have sex with you and move on to the next person and place? Jesus, Kat, who do you think I am? I'm not the sort of person who falls in love with anyone who passes by. I've never felt like this before you know."

Kat takes a bite out of her panini, saying in between chews, "Look, I'm a realist. You are young and beautiful and talented. You have many places to go and things to do. I'm not about to hold you back from any of it just because we had a nice few days together."

"Nice days together? You are unbelievable. So that's it? I see you've pretty much shut it down."

"I haven't done any such thing. I have enjoyed spending time with you, Julie. What I feel for you is incredibly powerful and I'm not going to pretend it's nothing, but I'm also not going to be that typical lesbian who wants to get a U-Haul and follow you around the world after a few days of great sex."

"Did Danielle hurt you this badly or was it someone else? Really, who was it? I want to know," Julie says, her voice rising.

"This isn't about who hurt me in the past. This is just reality. We are in very different places in our lives. That's it. It makes no sense to pretend otherwise." Kat's voice is steady, with hardly any intonation.

"Kat, that may be true, but it doesn't mean we don't see where this is going to go. I want to know you, really know you beyond what you show on the surface. Why can't that be enough for right now? Why can't we see where this goes? I don't know what happened between the YMCA and here in the last twenty minutes, but something changed you. You've shut down and I just don't get how you can do that." Julie moves closer and places her hand on Kat's thigh under the table. Kat jumps. "This. This is what I feel." Julie's hand travels up Kat's thigh to her crotch. She applies just enough pressure to make Kat squirm in her seat.

"Julie! Not here."

"You can't tell me this electricity between us is nothing. Now. We have to go now," Julie urges her.

Julie drops money on the table and rises to leave, even though both of them have barely touched their lunches. Kat feels this thunderstorm churning inside of her. She's worried, detached, and turned on simultaneously. But against her better judgment, she follows Julie out the door.

A few minutes later, after a silent but charged car ride during which neither one speaks or touches the other, Julie pushes her body against Kat as Kat tries to unlock the front door to her house.

"Hurry," whispers Julie as she bites Kat's ear. Kat moans at the touch. "I can't wait much longer." In a sudden burst, the door opens and they both nearly fall inside. Kat slams the door shut and Julie slams Kat against the back of the door. Her kisses are volatile and her tongue has an urgency all its own. Kat both responds and pulls back almost at the same time but she doesn't stop. She can't stop. If she can't tell her, she'll show her.

Julie's hands nearly tear at Kat's clothes. Her mouth covers every inch of exposed skin. The only thing keeping Kat upright is the pressure Julie is applying with her own body. Julie's fingers pull at the elastic band of Kat's sweats. She drops down on her knees, pulling Kat's pants down in one motion. Before Kat can protest, Julie's mouth is on her. Kat's body arches back against the door. Her left leg drapes over Julie's shoulder. Julie's tongue is on fire and her mouth pulls and sucks at Kat's clitoris harshly and without apology, with an insistence and intensity that overwhelms Kat's defenses.

"Oh. My. God. I'm coming. I'm going to come in

your mouth. Please don't stop." Kat's voice is ragged.

Julie's tongue caresses Kat, teasing her. Kat can feel Julie speaking with her lovemaking. With every touch and every kiss, Julie is breaking down every one of Kat's arguments. Kat's heart rate climbs and her vision blurs. Just a split second before the orgasm to end all orgasms explodes inside her, Julie stops. She rises so that she and Kat are eye to eye. Kat is totally bewildered and intensely aroused.

"Please, Julie," Kat moans desperately, "don't leave me like this."

Julie stands like that for what seems like an eternity and slowly, so slowly, moves her fingers inside Kat, cupping them forward. Kat's eyes widen. The pleasure pulls them both to a deep and intense place. With every thrust, Julie's hand moves deeper and deeper into Kat. Once again, only even stronger than before, Kat's orgasm builds. Kat knows that this is the moment she will remember forever whether their lives meld together or they go their separate ways.

Kat feels like she is above her body, looking down on herself and what Julie is doing to her. Somehow, Julie is on her G-spot as if she knows Kat's body better than her own. She hears the blood pulsing in her temples. When she opens her eyes, Julie is there, staring at her with those endlessly blue-green eyes. Kat starts to feel the tingle in her toes, her shoulders, her neck, and her fingers. Without warning the orgasm that overcomes her arches her back. Somewhere in the distance, she hears a guttural yell and vaguely realizes the sound is coming from her. The orgasm rocks her body with wave after wave until every thought in her mind is obliterated. Shockwaves pulse through Kat's body one after another until her body falls limp and used against

Julie. Kat tries to hold them back, but tears well in her eyes and slide slowly down her cheeks. Julie kisses the tears from her face.

"I'm not sad. Really. Just overwhelmed," whispers Kat.

"I know," Julie says as she kisses her lips. "I love you, Kat."

Part Two

Someday, somewhere—anywhere, unfailingly, you'll find yourself, and that, and only that, can be the happiest or bitterest hour of your life.
—Pablo Neruda

Chapter Fifteen

Kat props her feet up on the railing, staring out at Provincetown Bay and the beach at low tide. She leans back against the teakwood chair, taking a deep breath and filling her lungs with the sweet, salty early May air. Provincetown, Massachusetts is her new home since she abruptly moved here six months ago. Why she picked Provincetown out of anywhere in the country is a mystery even to her. She'd never set foot in town before but had heard it mentioned by many people over the years as artsy, very gay friendly, and beautiful.

She even broke down and adopted a young black lab-pit bull mix she named Cooper for WNBA legend Cynthia Cooper. Cooper snores contentedly by her feet. She flips open the laptop and keys a few search terms in. Moments later, she watches a preseason interview with the New York Liberty's most popular player, Julie Stevens. Julie talks about her excitement for the upcoming season. Kat tries to control the feelings, the pull from deep inside her as she watches Julie speak, but she's come to terms with the fact that no matter how much time passes, something within her will always lurch forward whenever she sees that beautiful face or hears her voice.

Satisfied she's caught up on everything Julie, Kat closes the laptop and looks out over the rolling blue waves of Provincetown Bay. Even though she and Molly just redecorated it, Kat just couldn't stand the sight of her own house in New York anymore. It was loaded with too many memories of Danielle, of Julie, and of her own shortcomings. Shortly after the last visit with Julie, Kat walked through her house room by room. She saw the color palette of the beach and realized the beach was exactly where she had to go. So she made an uncharacteristically sudden decision to put the house on the market. The house sold within a week for a sizeable profit and a quick closing. That enabled her to buy the small, single-story, weathered clapboard Cape house, sight unseen, on the beach at the East End of Provincetown—her own personal slice of heaven.

When she told Molly of her plans to quit officiating and move to Provincetown, her oldest friend was vocal about her doubts. "Why are you running away from your own life?" she asked Kat more than once. "You're walking away from everything you've worked so hard for. I'm here. Mom and Dad are here. Why would you leave?

"No," Kat said. "You know I love you guys, but a house is just a place to sleep. I have nothing here but memories. I want—no—I need a fresh start."

"But what about basketball? That's your home more than anything else," Molly said, pulling the basketball card as a last resort.

"No, it's not. Basketball is tainted for me now. I just don't love it like I did. And I can't be around her, Molly. I can't be there and pretend there's nothing between us."

Kat remembers the panic she felt her first week in P-Town, as the locals call it. The little house she purchased was in foreclosure. While the exterior just needed some TLC, the interior needed a lot of cosmetic work that Kat didn't necessarily know how to do. With the help of some local tradesman and YouTube, she ripped up carpet and laid down hardwood floors. She painted walls, refinished kitchen cabinets, and even replaced the kitchen countertop herself. She refinished the bathroom and installed a new toilet and vanity.

Now, six months after leaving her life, she sits back in an old Adirondack chair that came with the house, taking her first real break. This house is now hers and hers alone. It holds no one else's memories or expectations. She doesn't even bother installing a phone. She has a cell phone, basic cable, and Internet. That is enough.

Kat doesn't feel comfortable living too much longer on her savings so she begins asking around town for odd jobs. The beauty of a small town is that everyone knows everyone and the year-rounders are a close bunch who always stick together. They value their privacy but they also make sure to help one another because long after the throngs of summer tourists depart, they remain to weather the often-rough winters together. After a few inquiries, she meets with a local photographer looking for someone to run her photography gallery.

Kat's interview with Abby Carmichael, a tough-as-nails, fifty-something photographer with cropped salt-and-pepper hair, is unusual to say the least. Abby sizes her up in seconds, asking Kat if she has a problem with gay people.

Kat laughs. "I don't have a problem with gay people. I'm a lesbian myself."

"Got a problem with trannies?"

"Nope," Kat replies.

"Bears?"

"Nope."

"Baby dykes?" Abby asks.

"Um, nope."

"Well you should, they make a mess in town."

"Okay, I'll remember that," Kat says.

"What do you know about running a gallery?"

"Absolutely nothing. But I have a business degree from Notre Dame. I'm a hard worker and fast learner."

"What've you been doing since you graduated from college?"

"I've been a basketball official for the WNBA and Division One college basketball."

"Got any skeletons in your closet?" Abby asks, peering at Kat.

"More than a few."

Abby slams her hand down on the table. "How does thirty bucks an hour sound? No benefits."

"That sounds great."

"Summers are brutal, though. You'll be working a lot of hours, including evenings and weekends."

"That's fine."

"Great. So how 'bout you start Monday? Come by The Squealing Pig tonight for happy hour and I'll introduce you to a bunch of locals and Wellfleet oysters."

"Sure. That sounds great. Oh, one thing, Abby—I have a new dog. Any chance I can bring her to the gallery while I'm working so she doesn't have to be alone?"

Abby smiles for the first time. "That depends on what kind of dog she is."

"A black lab mix"

"Oh, thank God. If you told me you had a cockapoo or one of those drop-kick dogs, our deal would've been off. She calm?"

"Very. And great with people."

"Sure. See you tonight."

❧❧❧❧

Three weeks later, Kat and Cooper are settled into their new routine. Every morning she and Cooper go for a three-mile run on the beach together. She's beginning to understand the beauty of the off-season and looks forward to the days after the tourist season when she and Cooper will have the beach all to themselves. After their run, a shower, and breakfast, Kat and Cooper walk into town. It's only a mile to Abby's gallery and parking is always a nightmare, so walking really is the best option next to riding a bike, which is impossible with Cooper. Kat grabs a coffee at the Wired Puppy, where Cooper always gets a treat, and they open the gallery together by ten o'clock. Kat thinks about how she doesn't miss the constant shuffle and traveling from one place to another. She's more content here than she's been in a long, long time.

Usually, Kat has an hour or so of quiet at the gallery before tourists start walking around. She spends that time answering messages and making sure orders for prints and framed photos are packed and invoiced. A heavily tattooed young man named Jaden handles all the prints and framing. He rarely speaks and can always be seen bobbing his head in the back with his headphones on. Kat usually communicates with him by note or hand signal, which is fine by her. The work isn't tough but it takes organization.

Once the flow of tourists increases, her day shifts to customer service: she talks to potential buyers about Abby's work and her expertise with long-exposure landscapes. To Abby's credit, she spent a great deal of time explaining her craft to Kat, knowing it would be Kat on the front lines with the customers and she would need to be properly educated to do the work justice. Kat enjoys talking with people and finds the busy pace of the sweet summer town comforting. In the few short weeks Kat's been working there, Abby knows her gallery is in good hands, and she knows her work and the money are safe with Kat.

Every evening at six o'clock, an older woman named Joyce takes the evening shift until closing at nine-thirty p.m. Some nights, when it's busy, Kat will stay on, but most evenings she is free. She typically ends her day at The Squealing Pig—a great little Irish pub with the best oysters in town—for a beer and a quick dinner at the bar. Sometimes, Abby meets her there and the two laugh and talk long into the evening.

One night, the bar is relatively quiet and Kat is in a particularly pensive mood. She knows she's PMSing, but still, she's moody and she can feel it.

"So when are you going to let me shoot you and Cooper?" Abby asks.

"Whenever. You tell me."

"Let's try Friday. If the weather holds, the sunset should be spectacular. We can go out by Race Point."

"Sure. That sounds great. I'm sure Cooper will love to see the seals."

"I'm not the type of person to ask too many questions—"

"Really? Are you kidding me?" Kat interrupts her. "I don't think so. My interview with you was a firing squad of questions."

"That doesn't count. I'm supposed to ask questions in an interview. That's the whole point of an interview for Christ's sakes. Anyway, as I was saying before you rudely interrupted me, I was about to ask why you aren't with anyone."

"Well, that's a loaded question."

"I've got nowhere to be," Abby says as she waves the bartender James for another round of beer.

At first, Kat's instinct is to pass the comment off and leave, which she knows is typical for her, but she decides to tell Abby her story—all of it. She tells her about her mother, about Danielle, and about Julie. She talks about how Molly and her family saved her. She doesn't gloss over the details and she's surprised at how much she actually shares with Abby. After she's done, she leans back in the bar stool and thinks that it's the first time she's talked to anyone like this with the exception of Molly. It feels good to be so honest and open with another person.

Abby doesn't say much, but she listens to all of it. After a while, she says, "You know a lot of people come out here to P-Town to leave another life behind. I've lived here my whole life, but I can see why you'd want a clean start. Sometimes, we have to walk away from what is comfortable to make peace with ourselves."

"Honestly, Abby, that's it exactly. I just want peace. My whole life I've been pushing and struggling to be respected—despite my mother—to make something of myself. Everything I did, I fought for. And when I thought I found someone to make a life with, I was wrong. I'm just tired in my soul."

"You need time to heal."

"Yeah, how much time you think that will take?"

"We have a saying out here: 'only the ocean knows for sure.'"

"So why aren't you with anyone?" Kat asks.

"Oh me? I'm an open book. The love of my life, Elise, died three years ago of ovarian cancer. It was nasty. I'm tellin' you, if I ever get sick like that I'll end things myself before it turns into that. Watching someone you love wither away and die is just about the worst thing you can ever experience. We were together for almost twenty-seven years and now that she's gone, I'm not really interested in trying to find someone to fill the hole she left. I'm content with my work, and my life here is full of friends and people I love. And Lord knows I'm too old to start dating again."

"If my friend Molly was here she'd say you are never too old to start dating again."

"My heart just isn't in it," Abby says, "and I'm beyond it."

"Well let's toast to finding peace," Kat says as she lifts her glass to Abby's.

Chapter Sixteen

One morning, Kat arrives at the gallery surprised to see Abby there before her.

"Wow! You are here early. What's the occasion?"

Abby calls Kat over to the large worktable in the back of the gallery. "I've got something I need you to approve."

Perplexed, Kat walks to the back of the gallery. A dozen large prints of her and Cooper are spread out across the worktable. Some are just of her looking out at the water. Even Kat can't deny the haunting quality of the images. When she went with Abby to Race Point for the photo session, she half believed it was a joke. She never thought the photos would actually amount to anything useful.

"You lied. You said you specialized in landscapes."

"I thought so too," says Abby. "But you can't deny it—these are kind of amazing."

"Part of me is embarrassed, but part of me knows you've really captured me, and, of course, Cooper!" Cooper wags her tail at the sound of her name.

There is one image in particular that Kat can't take her eyes off of. It's a profile of her staring out at the sunset with the wind blowing her black hair back off her face and shoulders. Abby sees the picture she's fixed on.

"That one. I agree. I don't know where you were in your mind when I took that picture, but it's all there in your face and in the ocean at the same time. It's like you are mirroring each other. Kat, if it's okay with you, I want to feature this one in the gallery. Of course, you'll get the first numbered print and I'll frame it for you free of charge."

"That's very kind of you, Abby, but it's a little weird to hang a large print of myself at my house. It seems a little narcissistic."

"Well, I'll hold it aside for you and you can take it when you want, okay?"

"Sure, okay."

"And I'd like to pay you a bonus for being the subject. We'll work something out once we get through the summer."

"That's very generous, thanks."

A few days later, Kat's photo is featured in the front window of the gallery. She knows the photo is making an impression because both visitors and overall sales have increased quite a bit since it's gone up. Usually, people stare at the photo and do a double take when they see Kat working in the store. More than one woman propositions Kat too, although she politely turns her down. The print quickly becomes one of Abby's best sellers.

The summer continues to fly by in a whirl of activity. June gets busier and July is crazy in town and inside the gallery. Kat and Cooper become accustomed to dodging the bikes, cars, pedestrians, and pedicabs jammed on Commercial Street. The town is usually buzzing in the morning and quiet during the hot afternoons while everyone is at the beach, but once five o'clock hits, the town begins filling up until the early hours of the morning. Because of the change in activity, Kat switches her time at the gallery. She takes a few hours off in the midafternoon while Joyce takes a shift, happy to be in an air-conditioned space. Kat usually returns around six and stays on until late closing at eleven p.m.

During her time off, she hits the beach too. Sometimes, she lets Cooper stay in the air-conditioned gallery or she will take her to play in the water, careful to keep her under an umbrella to stay cool. Kat can't imagine what her life was like before having Cooper. The dog's sweet nature calms her and helps keep her grounded. She has to admit, Molly is right. There is something to be said for a living creature always happy to see you no matter how you look or feel.

This afternoon, Kat leaves Cooper home in the air conditioning while she spends some time soaking up the sun at Herring Cove Beach. While there are no actual markers, the beach tends to break up into groups. The lesbians, who usually have loads of gear, tents, and coolers, pick spots closest to the parking lot path. Then the gay men are next in their little speedos. The far end of the beach is a free-for-all where folks go nude when the mood strikes them. Kat usually tries to find a spot on the far right end of the beach as the dune curves around, giving her the most privacy. Today she finds a good spot, but the beach is crowded and she's feeling uncomfortable at all the eyes watching her pull off her white tank top to show off her black bikini and toned body.

She tries to ignore the open stares from women on all sides and goes for a swim in the water, which is still pretty chilly, while staring up at the beautiful, sharp blue sky and perfectly white clouds. All of the beach plums and wild roses are in full bloom and dot the edges of the beach with their reddish, purple flowers. It is a spectacular summer day—the kind of day you try to recall in the middle of February when everything is gray and wet and cold.

Kat allows her whole body to float close to shore. It happens the way it always does. She closes her eyes and involuntarily shudders at the memory of their lovemaking or the way Julie looked at her when she said she loved her. She pushes the memory from her mind and emerges from the water, aware that several women stare at her glistening and very tan body as she walks back up the beach to the privacy of her headphones. Even though she rarely listens to music at the beach, preferring to listen to the sound of the seagulls and waves, she uses the headphones as a deterrent to conversation and pickup lines that she has no use for.

Today, in particular, the weight of the world is on her mind. Even the blue-green water reminds her of Julie's eyes. Some days are worse than others and she's used to that by now. She's learned to cope by shoving the feelings down and out of anyone's reach, but she recognizes that with all the walls and protections up, she is getting lonely. It's been ten months since that last day with Julie. Ten months since her body and soul were connected completely to someone else. Ten months or a lifetime, take your pick.

One of the things Kat is learning about herself is the way she closes herself off to the world around her. It's involuntary, like holding in a sneeze, but it's a self-protection mechanism. She knows the damage her father's leaving did to her, even though she never really knew him. She's perfectly aware of the damage her alcoholic mother did to her in her formative years; no amount of time with a therapist will make her see that any clearer than she already does. She was eight years old the last time she actually remembers being hugged by her mother, and even then, she can't quite remember if her mother was drunk or sober.

Before Kat's mother died, she felt responsible for taking care of her, for being the adult, the breadwinner, and the mature one. After she died, she just carried that responsibility onto herself. Her hard work on the basketball court landed her that full ride to Notre Dame, which she never really gave herself the space to appreciate or enjoy.

Some people think athletes like Kat are just born with boatloads of natural talent and everything they do on the court or the track or the field just comes as naturally as breathing, but that's far from the case. Sure, Kat knows she possesses genetic athletic ability, but what she has that many other athletes never possess is the willingness to do the work that it takes to become great, no matter how uncomfortable that work might be. Kat took her job as a basketball player seriously. She put in the extra time before and after practice to improve herself. She spent hours studying film when everyone else was out having fun.

The thought occurs to her that for as long as she can remember, she's been working. Hard. She held down multiple jobs all while going to school, playing basketball, and caring for her mother and their home in high school. She played Division I college basketball in an elite program as a scholarship player for four years, which in itself is a full-time job. And, in addition, she carried an honors course load and worked part-time. After college and a bunch of failed tryouts for professional teams, she threw herself completely into becoming the best official she could be, working her way slowly up the ladder to the elite WNBA and Division I NCAA women's basketball, until Julie.

Something snapped in her that last day with Julie when they made love up against her front door. She felt the twinge like a rubber band breaking. She knew that first moment her eyes locked onto Julie on the basketball court, of all places, her life would be irrevocably changed. The day Julie left her house, Kat knew she would shut her out of her life, even though every fiber of her being was aching to tell her to stay. Julie had growing up to do. She had a life to live and basketball to play in the US and around the world. It's not the kind of life you just walk away from because you meet someone special; it's the kind of life you make sacrifices for because it is such a gift. After all, sacrifice is the mother of all accomplishments. Kat's dream was to play professional basketball and she's always wondered if she didn't sacrifice enough to achieve it. She could never forgive herself if she was somehow the cause of taking that beautiful gift away from Julie. And so, she watched Julie walk out her front door and jump into a taxi. Kat promised herself that she would not need her. She might want her, she might miss her, but she would not foist her need upon Julie even if Julie felt she could handle it or somehow wanted it. Because the void her parents left within her, the void she's felt since Danielle walked out, that void can't be filled by anyone else. It's something she has to do herself.

That's why her sudden move to the Cape felt like life or death to Kat. She knew that if she stayed in that house another month, what was left of her soul would wither and die. Her trusty self-protection mechanism sent her to the beach because somewhere deep down, she knew that if she didn't make healing herself her number one priority, there would be nothing left for

Julie or anyone else to love.

The problem for Kat has always been her inability to get out of her own head and share these complex feelings with someone else. She knows she should have told Julie all of this, but time has a way of making all decisions easier to understand and back then, Kat just couldn't find the words to tell Julie all she was feeling. The vortex of emotions was more than she could bear and she just wasn't in a place to articulate them to anyone else, least of all Julie who had caused the dam to break to begin with.

To say that Kat isn't proud of the way things ended with Julie is an understatement. The way she walked away is something she knows she'll regret for the rest of her life, but it was a decision she had to make in the moment. On a day like this, when the sun is warm on her body and the sky looks so open and clear, hope is not difficult to find or feel. Somewhere deep inside, she hopes that she will have the chance to make things right with Julie. She hopes there will be a day when the stars align and they can come back into each other's lives, but she also realizes that she wasn't able to give what Julie wanted from her. Maybe if there ever is a next time, she will be ready. For now, this beautiful day, her dog Cooper, her new life in Provincetown has to be enough.

Chapter Seventeen

Julie readjusts the towel she's using as a pillow against the window of the charter bus. It's raining outside, the kind of pounding, pelting rain that seeps its dampness into your bones even if you're dry, even though it's a hot mid-July day. Her headphones are on, blasting her ritual pregame playlist, but instead of listening to the words of Eminem and getting juiced up for tonight's game against Connecticut, she's wondering if she ever crosses Kat's mind.

Julie knows this kind of thinking isn't productive. Her Jedi ability to tune out the world when she sets foot on a court is her salvation. The forty minutes of the game is the only true reprieve she has. Every other waking—and sometimes sleeping—moment is centered on Kat and only Kat

She tries to align her thinking to the game at hand by staring at the stat sheets half crumpled in her palm. After a stellar season in Italy, her numbers back in the WNBA for a new season are at career highs and at all-star-level caliber for the entire league. She's shooting 54 percent from beyond the arc. That's a career best for her. Ninety-seven percent from the free-throw line. Also a career best. Averaging 19.7 points per game along with six rebounds, five assists, and two turnovers. She's playing nearly thirty-seven to thirty-eight minutes per game. Her body is strong and healthy, but the mental fatigue she feels at every turn is very real. Her brain is toast and she knows it.

She stuffs the stat sheets in her bag and checks her cell phone. Checking her cell phone for text messages from Kat that she knows will never come is now an hourly ritual bordering on sickness. So does checking Kat's Facebook page, which has been dormant for ten months, although sometimes she scrolls through the old photos of Kat just to keep the memory of her near. She knows she can't do that now. They'll be pulling up to the Mohegan Sun arena in less than thirty minutes. She knows if she looks at a picture of Kat with her shining black hair and those smoky eyes that simultaneously show and hide so much of her soul, she'll be useless for this game, and her teammates need her A-game tonight. So, Julie closes her eyes, letting the rock and bounce of the bus take her away from the broken record that keeps playing over and over in her mind.

An hour later, Melanie, the athletic trainer, tapes her left ankle. Melanie seems to be happy every waking moment of every day. Julie still hasn't figured out of it's an act or if she really is that genuinely and ridiculously happy.

"Is that too tight?" Melanie asks, noticing Julie's calf muscle tighten up.

"No, it's good. Last time it was too loose."

"Do you want your right ankle taped?"

"No, I think I'm good. It feels fine."

"Okay, well, let's check again at halftime to be sure."

Julie carefully pulls on her socks, slips on her sneakers, and slides off the training table. Ever since freshman year in college, she has not actually laced up her sneakers until she gets out on the floor. Every player has idiosyncratic rituals they swear make them lucky or play better. This one is nonnegotiable for Julie, and her teammates know it. They also know she has to sit in the third chair from the end of the bench to lace up and they always leave that spot free for her.

She sits down in her designated seat and slowly starts tightening her laces from the toes up. Her teammates stretch, shoot, and go through their own pregame rituals too. The time before warm-ups is sacred to a player. No fans are allowed in the arena yet. The music is loud with songs the players want to hear instead of the repetitive fan favorites, and the atmosphere is relaxed. Players from opposing teams often loosen up together and chat. Julie has never been a big talker during this part of pregame. She finishes lacing up and spends about five minutes dribbling a ball. She loves waking her hands up to the feeling of the ball and getting a sense for how the hardwood is reacting and how high or low the balls are inflated.

The officiating crew make their way onto the floor, starting their own version of warm-ups. Julie spots Deb who casually strolls over to her to repeat the same conversation they have every time they see one another before or after a game.

"Heard from her yet?" asks Deb.

"Nothing. You?" replies Julie.

"Nope. Have a good game, kid. Light 'em up."

"Thanks, Deb."

After Kat shut Julie out of her life, Julie reached out to Deb for some advice but the steely referee had little to offer her.

"Kat's a tough nut to crack, kiddo. She's never been very predictable, which is one of the things I love about her. I don't know what to tell you. We're all as surprised as you are. Not only did she shut you out, but she shut me out too. She took a leave of absence as an official."

"Leave of absence?" Julie was stunned when she learned this. "But how could she? Basketball is her life. She would never walk away from the game. She loves it too much."

"Apparently, you're wrong on that score, kiddo. She did walk away. Not much notice either. She told everyone she was burned out and needed some time to reevaluate what she wanted from life. I don't even know where she's at."

"I've been texting her. I even sent her mail, but it got sent back," Julie says.

"I got no response when I emailed her either," says Deb. "For all I know, she clean fell off the side of the earth."

Julie goes through the motions of warm-ups knowing she's in a strange mental frame of mind. She's fuzzy, she's mixed up, and she's unable to "clear the mechanism" as Kevin Costner says in the movie *For the Love of the Game*. Before she really has a chance to concentrate, she's sitting on the bench, hearing her name being called; it echoes as though she's in a long tunnel. She rises, jogging to center court and slapping her teammates' outstretched hands.

The announcer's deep voice rebounds off the hardwood: "At guard, from the University of Connecticut, Julie Stevens." She vaguely registers the sound of the Connecticut crowd giving her a warm welcome. Connecticut fans are the best. They always cheer on their Huskies, even if a former Husky plays on an opposing team. She knows that's why the crowd is a little better than average tonight.

The lights shut off and the Connecticut

introductions start, swirling the fans into a loud tip-off cheer. Julie sits down in her seat as one of the five starters. She towels off her face and hands, waiting for the lights to go back on so they can get final instructions from Coach Clery.

A few minutes later, she stands at center court, facing the New York rim. For some reason, the thought occurs to her that Kat might be in the crowd. This isn't a typical thought for her moments before tip-off, and it rattles her. The tip comes her way but she is so lost in thought that she bobbles it, causing an immediate turnover and Connecticut's first points of the game.

"Get your head in the game," yells Coach Clery from the sideline. Julie takes one last look at the crowd near center court, quickly scanning for Kat's face. She sees nothing but strangers staring back. Then suddenly, she flips the switch. She clears the mechanism. Her mind is no longer anywhere else but within the lines of the court. She locks into the sound the ball makes on the hardwood. She hears the sneakers squeaking. She can feel her own heart beating and she can hear her own breathing. Then the dance begins.

For the next thirty-nine minutes, Julie Stevens puts up a performance for the ages. This is the kind of game that isn't just talked about in the WNBA, it's talked about on ESPN and every sports talk show around the country as one of the most dominant performances by a basketball player male or female—ever. Julie doesn't just score points; she single-handedly annihilates Connecticut. She hits a staggering eight three-pointers, missing only once in the first quarter for the entire game. From the floor, she nails another eleven points, missing just two jumpers. One hundred percent and six points from the line for a total of forty-one points.

Forty-one points on only three misses, along with nine rebounds, four assists, and one turnover. It's a career-best game for her.

Her anger at Kat pours out of her in a way that is otherworldly. Every v-cut is a tear she shed over Kat. Every box out is an opportunity for someone else to feel her pain. Every three-pointer and jump shot is a chance to inflict damage. And tonight, she pours the tattered pieces of her broken heart out onto the floor for everyone to see. This isn't just a statement game. This is a purging, an emptying of every solitary emotion she's kept bottled up since the day Kat closed her front door and shut Julie out of her life. Julie channels all of the negative emotions—the pain, the heartache, the sadness, and the loneliness—all of it, into her game. It makes no difference which player is chosen to guard her. It's not about them. It's about her. They are just in the way, conveniently placed there for her to utterly and completely destroy.

No one dares to speak with her at halftime. This is another unwritten rule of the game. When a player is hot in the first half, you leave her completely alone in the locker room for fear she will cool off in the second half. Her teammates give her a wide berth and Coach Clery doesn't even mention her name. Melanie, the trainer, doesn't ask Julie about her ankle taping. Everyone respects the fact that Julie is on track for the kind of game that will go down in history and no one wants to be the schmuck who screws it up.

At some point during the second half, Julie looks up at the clock. She sees the numbers 21–79. That can't be right, she thinks. She knows she recognizes the numbers, but from where? Then it hits her. That's how many points Kat scored in high school. Kat. That day they made love against Kat's front door and the whole universe opened up to let them both in. Julie blinks back tears. She looks up at the clock again but the numbers are gone, replaced instead by the actual score of the game: 51–39. She feels panic well up inside of her and shoves it aside. The ball is thrown to her on the left wing. She stops thinking. Pump fake, jab step, one dribble to the left, and a floating, singularly beautiful arc, and the ball falls through the hoop barely making contact with the net. She sees Deb signal a three-pointer. The sound from the crowd is muffled. She can feel blood coursing in her neck and the sweat as it drips down her back. She does not smile, but with each made shot, her scowl grows bolder, fiercer.

After the final buzzer sounds, after the group team hug, after the Connecticut fans give her a wildly appreciative standing ovation, after the boring postgame pretend-to-be-ecstatic interviews and press conference, after the shower, Julie readjusts the towel she's using as a pillow against the window of the charter bus on the return trip back to New York. It's still raining outside, and she wonders if she will feel this hollow for the rest of her life.

Chapter Eighteen

Kat watches Julie's epic game on replay four times over the next three weeks. It wasn't a joyful performance by Julie. It was the kind of performance only a broken heart can cause, and Kat knows it. She registers the tears streaming down Julie's face when she stares up at the clock at the beginning of the second half. She sees the expression on Julie's face that is both a mask and mirror, hiding and releasing so much pain. Kat watches every moment of that game knowing it was a message, a lifeline to her, and it's more than she can bear. She closes the laptop and whistles for Cooper. She needs the beach. Now.

Five minutes later, she and Cooper walk on the serene expanse of beach, but Kat doesn't even have the energy to walk very far. She just drops down in the sand and stares at the water. *How could I inflict so much pain on someone I love so much?* That thought rattles around in her mind. That's what she can't seem to shake. She was doing Julie a favor. She was setting her free instead of tying her down, instead of jeopardizing her career. She never meant to hurt her, and she never dreamed she would wound her so deeply. This isn't the kind of thing you are forgiven for. This is the kind of broken heart that one doesn't ever recover from. This is the kind of broken heart that dulls every emotion and sheds the warmth of the sun.

Kat is so utterly lost in thought she doesn't see or

hear someone walk up next to her.

"Excuse me."

"Oh, sorry, what?" says Kat, bewildered.

"Hi. Sorry to disturb. I was just wondering if you knew the time."

Kat stares blankly at the face in front of her before responding. "Well, it has to be five o'clock somewhere."

The woman laughs, a lyrical and light sound, snapping Kat out of her own mind.

"That's the truth. Does that mean we can have a cocktail?"

Kat smiles. The woman smiles back. Kat notices her freckles and the French braid of auburn hair wrapped over her left shoulder. What a pretty smile, she thinks. What kind eyes.

"Are you okay? You seem to be a little out of sorts," the woman says gently.

"Um, yeah. Sorry, it's the ocean. Sometimes it just sucks me in," Kat says, doing her best to pull herself together.

"Ah, yeah, I know what you mean."

Kat scrambles to her feet and wipes the sand from her legs. When she stands straight, she notices the woman is her same height (which is not typical for Kat) and is still staring at her with an open, kind expression. The wisps of hair pulled loose from her braid blow in the breeze. The woman smiling back is a little younger than Kat, but not by much. Her dark, alluring eyes and openness knock Kat momentarily off guard. Cooper nudges at the stranger for an introduction.

"Oh, sorry, this is Cooper. She likes to be properly introduced."

"Hi, Cooper. I'm Antonia." She drops down on one knee and shakes Cooper's outstretched paw, instantly becoming a favorite friend. She rises and extends her hand to Kat.

"Sorry, I thought I should shake with Cooper first."

"Oh, that's fine. Cooper prefers it that way. I'm Kat. Nice to meet you."

As Kat and Antonia shake hands, Kat notices Antonia's long slender fingers and is surprised to see so many freckles.

"Are you here on vacation?" asks Kat politely as the two disengage their hands a little reluctantly.

"Yes. No. Well, sort of."

It's not a complicated question.

Antonia laughs. "I'm a writer. I just needed to get away to finish a project and thought this would be a quiet place to write."

"You definitely picked the wrong place. P-Town in August is anything but quiet."

"Yes, I'm getting that." Antonia smirks. "I booked a room in the center of town and am quickly realizing it doesn't quiet down until about four in the morning."

"The next couple of weeks are really hectic with Carnival coming up."

"I saw that. What is it?"

"It's only one of the biggest and gayest week-long parties in the country, capped off by one of the biggest gay-pride parades, or, at least, that's what I'm told. It'll be my first one this year."

"Oh, I had no idea. I thought it was some kids' event—you know like a carnival with rides and cotton candy," Antonia says, shrugging.

"Yeah, you got that really wrong. From what I gather, you'll probably see cotton candy, but it'll be duct taped to someone as an edible outfit for the parade." Kat grins.

Antonia laughs. "Now that's an image."

"You must not be from around here. Everyone from New York to Boston knows about Provincetown's infamous Carnival week."

"No, actually I'm from just outside of Cleveland."

"And you needed more quiet than that to write?"

"You'd think it's quiet enough but, well, it's a long story. Family stuff," Antonia responds.

"Ahh."

The two stand for a few moments, a little expectant and uncomfortably quiet. Kat breaks the silence first. "I've got to run. I have to work this evening so I'd better get going."

"Oh, sure. Where do you work?" Antonia asks.

"Carmichael Gallery just past MacMillan Wharf."

"I know that place. I keep meaning to stop in every time I walk by. Beautiful landscape photography, right?"

"Right. You should stop by. I'm usually there most days until one and evenings," says Kat, a little surprised she is volunteering so much information.

"I will. Thanks. Nice to meet you, Cooper," says Antonia as she pats Cooper on the head. "And you too, Kat. What's Kat short for?"

"Katherine."

"With a K or a C?" she asks.

"A K. Why?"

Just wondering."

"Right. The writer," Kat says as she walks away with Cooper. A few paces down the beach, Kat looks down at Cooper. "Well that was interesting, wasn't it, Cooper?" She turns quickly to catch a glimpse of Antonia and is surprised to see her standing in the same spot on the beach, watching Kat.

Chapter Nineteen

The next day is brutally hot: the kind of hot that makes one wish for winter...the kind of hot that makes it difficult to breathe. Kat is relieved to be in the cool gallery today and has no desire to go to the beach. Abby's gallery is doing extremely well this summer, so well in fact that prints are flying out almost faster than Jaden can make them. But P-town is dead today because everyone else is either inside or at the beach, so Kat takes advantage of the quiet time to reorganize the gallery, restock the print boxes, check emails, and get the books updated.

With her mind buried in sales figures, Kat doesn't even hear the jingle of the door as it opens. She hears someone cough lightly and jumps to her feet in surprise only to see Antonia gazing at her with that same kind and warm smile she remembers from their meeting on the beach the day before. Cooper is already wagging her tail at Antonia, clearly remembering her new friend.

"Well, hello there," Kat says. "You're out braving the heat, I see." Kat notices Antonia's face is flushed from the heat.

"Not really braving it, just strategically avoiding it. I figured a little shopping was in order since all the stores are air conditioned."

"Good thinking. How's the writing coming?"

"Oh, well, awful actually. I had big plans to get all this writing done but I'm not really writing anything."

"Ahh, it's the beach."

"What do you mean?" Antonia asks.

"The beach will keep you from doing anything but nothing."

"That's exactly it! I feel like I'm not doing anything productive but then at night, I'm wiped out and sleeping better than I have in forever."

"Yeah, it's the salt air. Something about it makes everything else seem pretty insignificant."

"Well you're working, so at least someone is being productive." Antonia glances down at Kat's tidy workspace.

"This is the first quiet day we've had in weeks. It's actually kind of nice to get caught up. Listen, can you give me a second just to close out of this document? I want to make sure I save everything."

"Sure, absolutely. So sorry to bother you." Antonia steps back and begins looking at large-format prints around the gallery.

"You're not bothering me at all. Just one sec." Kat sits back down, cleaning up her files and saving the Excel document she was working on. She takes a moment to watch Antonia, noting which prints she stops to look at. As Kat takes in the sight of her in her khaki shorts and white tank top, she senses something earthy and warm. Antonia exudes a quiet, competent sexiness that Kat's never quite noticed in another woman before. She's drawn to it.

Antonia looks intently at the picture Abby took of Kat as Kat walks up to her.

"I'm still a little embarrassed to see that shot every day when I come in. I try to ignore it."

"Oh, no? Why? It's truly amazing. There's something eerie and haunting about the way the light of the sunset is captured. And well, you look beautiful," Antonia says, sounding almost a little surprised. "Wait, that sounded wrong. Not like you're not beautiful now, it's just…oh gosh, I've really dug myself a hole on this one, haven't I?" She blushes.

Kat squints her eyes mischievously, amused at Antonia's discomfort. "Not at all. I know what you mean. Sometimes, I look at it and I don't even think it looks like me at all."

"Well, that's the thing. It looks like the essence of you or something."

"Oh, I don't know. I wouldn't go that far. So, what is it you're writing?

"You mean not writing," Antonia says.

"Right or supposed to be writing."

"A play."

"Are there many playwrights in Cleveland?"

"No, hardly any, actually. But almost six months ago, I received a fellowship from the Cleveland Playhouse and I'm way, way behind."

"Wow, that's fantastic. Congratulations!"

"Thanks."

Several shoppers enter the store, immediately changing the energy between the two.

"Excuse me, I'm here to pick up a photograph," says a young man.

"Oh sure. C'mon back to the counter," Kat says to him. Before she moves on, she turns toward Antonia shrugging apologetically. "I've got to run."

"Right. Of course. It was nice chatting with you. I'll leave you to it."

"Wait, what are you doing tonight?"

"Um, clearly we've established this. Nothing, why?"

"How about meeting me for dinner? You haven't told me what your play is about," Kat says, "and I have the evening off."

Antonia blushes again and smiles. "I'd like that."

"Great. Let's meet at Napi's. It's a great Portuguese restaurant just down the street. Let's say eight o'clock this evening?"

"Sure. See you later."

As Kat watches Antonia exit, she catches the curve of her hips as she moves. She makes a mental note to call in a favor with the manager at Napi's in order to get that reservation, looking more forward to the evening than she wants to admit to herself.

Chapter Twenty

Kat checks her wristwatch, surprised Antonia is fifteen minutes late. The white Christmas lights and dark wood paneling create a festive and cozy atmosphere, even in the middle of summer. The place is jammed, as she expected. Napi's is always busy. After uncharacteristically changing her clothes three times before her date, Kat finally settled on white slacks and a black tank top. She sits at the corner table and alternates between people watching and checking the door. As she sips her martini, she tries to pinpoint why she's so nervous. Then it hits her—it's been around nine years since she's asked a woman out on an actual bona fide date. This is also the first time in a long while that she feels comfortable in her own skin and secure enough to take the lead with someone who interests her.

Antonia blows in like a mini-hurricane, immediately ending Kat's internal musings. She spots Kat and hurries over, accidently knocking into two chairs on her way.

"I'm so, so sorry," she says, the words coming out in a rush as she sits down across from Kat. Antonia wears a pretty red-and-yellow sundress that sets off her hair and eyes perfectly. The fact that Kat is sitting with one of the most beautiful women in the room isn't lost on her. "I had some family issues to take care of and everything seems to take twice as long by phone."

"It's okay. Take a deep breath. Everything is fine."

Kat's tone is warm and caring.

Antonia sighs, leaning back in her chair as the tension in her face dissipates. "Yes, you're right. Relax. I have to tell myself to relax."

"You look lovely."

Antonia blushes. "Thanks. So do you." She looks around the restaurant. "This place is so cool inside. Very different from what I thought it'd look like."

"That's why I like it too. That and their food is great."

The waitress approaches, asking Antonia what she'd like to drink.

"I'll have a martini too. A little dirty, extra olives please."

The waitress nods and walks away.

"So," says Kat.

"So," says Antonia, smiling.

"How did the rest of your day go? Did you get any writing done?"

"Hardly. After I left the gallery, I decided it was too hot to do anything except get an ice cream cone and take a nap inside. I slept until about six o'clock and then all hell broke loose at home." Kat notices that every time Antonia mentions home, her brow furrows right down the center as if she's deep in concentration.

"Is everything okay now?" Kat asks as the waitress delivers Antonia's martini. "Wait one second. Don't answer that yet. Mind if I order a couple of apps?"

"No, perfect, go right ahead."

"Anything you don't like?"

"Nope, I'll try whatever."

"Okay. We'll have the crab cakes and pita with hummus to start."

"Terrific. I'll go put those in and give you time to

decide on your entrees," the waitress says.

"So, you were saying?" Kat asks.

"The truth is, I have two very sick parents that I take care of and while I wanted this trip to write, I also needed some time to myself. It's been a rough road. You know, to be honest, I'd rather not talk about it. I know that probably sounds totally selfish, but I just don't want to think about them tonight. Does that make me a bad person?" Antonia asks.

"No, I don't think that makes you a bad person at all. I get it."

Antonia takes a long sip of her martini. "In fact, this martini is so perfect I may just get drunk tonight.

"Oh boy. Well, pace yourself. I don't want to peel you off the floor." Kat's eyes crinkle in amusement.

"So, what about you? Are you originally from the Cape?"

"No, hardly," Kat says. "I grew up in Nebraska. I lived in New York up until five months ago. That's when I came here to P-Town, sight unseen."

"Really? I'm shocked! You seem so comfortable here."

"Well, I am comfortable here, but it's been a total change of pace from everything I was used to."

"Which was what?"

"Hmm, let's see. I had a house just north of New York City. I traveled a lot. Actually, I traveled all the time. I was a professional basketball official."

"Wow. Like in the WNBA?"

"Yes," Kat replies.

"Very cool. And you aren't anymore?"

"I sort of am. I took a leave of absence from my job but if I wait another season to come back, my career will basically be over. Although at this point, I don't think I even care." Kat shrugs and takes a long sip of her martini.

The waitress delivers the appetizers and both women immediately dig in.

"Well that's not what I expected at all," says Antonia. "It's not every day you meet a gorgeous professional basketball official who just up and leaves a career to run an art gallery in Provincetown."

"Gorgeous?"

"Um have you looked in the mirror lately?"

Kat can feel herself blushing and is thoroughly enjoying being flirted with.

"I know. I've never really been very conventional, though."

Antonia grins. "That must be nice. I've always been conventional. Boring. The good kid who never got into trouble, who has the responsibility for her family, who does what's expected."

"That can't be easy, but at least you have your parents. Mine are both gone. Have been for a long time," Kat says wistfully.

"My mom is as good as gone. She has advanced Alzheimer's. I'm lucky if she remembers the day of the week, let alone who I am. Lately, she's taken to calling me Jimmy and telling me my dad is trying to molest her." Antonia's smile doesn't reach her eyes.

"What do you say we don't talk about our troubles and we just enjoy the food and the martinis and each other's company?" Kat raises her glass in a toast.

"To living in the moment," says Antonia.

"To living in the moment."

≈≈≈≈≈

After stuffing themselves with a delicious dinner, Antonia and Kat walk down Commercial Street headed toward the East End. It's a warm night but the breeze off the ocean makes being outside a summertime treat all its own. The night sky is filled with bright stars and the smell of honeysuckle and the ocean permeates the air.

"I love walking Commercial Street at night," Kat says thoughtfully. "There's something so great about being able to look into people's houses. It's weirdly comforting."

"And not at all weirdly voyeuristic."

"No, not at all!"

The two walk in silence for a few minutes, taking in the beauty of the evening as the scorching heat of the day diminishes and fades out into the ocean.

"I've had a really nice time tonight," Antonia says.

"Me too."

"But I need to know something," Antonia continues.

"Hmm?"

"Was this a date? I mean, I can't really tell. I don't even know if you're gay or not. It's fine if this isn't or you're not, but it's also great actually if you are and this is, since I am. I'm just well—I'd be interested to know what this is, that's all."

"You know, you tend to ramble when you get nervous."

"I know I do. It's so embarrassing. I'm sure I'm also blushing but at least you can't see that in the dark."

"Well, to answer your questions, I am gay. I'm not sure if this was a date or not, either. It's been a very long time since I was out on a real date. So long, in fact, that I've sort of forgotten how it all works. All I know is I have really enjoyed spending time with you tonight,"

Kat tries to explain.

"Okay, then. That works." Antonia's voice softens.

"Good, I'm glad we got that settled. Look, I need to get back to Cooper before I have a full-blown mutiny on my hands. I had a great time with you too."

Antonia quickly kisses Kat on the cheek and heads back up Commercial Street.

"Good night. And thanks again."

"So will I see you around?"

"I know where to find you," says Antonia as she slips out of sight into the darkness.

Kat turns toward home and fills her lungs with the nighttime salt air, surprised at how light and carefree she feels.

Chapter Twenty-one

Julie is being fucked. Hard. But she doesn't feel a thing. She tries to clear the mechanism but apparently, that seems to only work on the basketball court. This is the first time she doesn't even care who she is with or where she is. She registers the time on the clock as 3:23 a.m. and thinks the woman whose head is between her legs is named Laurie or maybe it's Lillian. What does it matter, really?

Everything after the stunning game at the Mohegan Sun shifted for Julie. Her play has been downright incredible. She found the formula: pain equals performance, but after pouring so much of herself and her emotions onto the court night after night, she is empty inside whenever there is no basketball to be played. She mistakenly thought a one-night stand would do her good and make her feel like herself again, but all it's doing is making her feel less like herself…less of anything really.

"Look, this isn't going to happen for me tonight, I'm sorry," Julie says abruptly.

The woman looks up at Julie a little surprised to be stopped midway.

"Am I doing something wrong?" the woman asks, slinking up Julie's body. Julie sits upright, grabbing the covers close.

"No, it's not you. It's me. My head's just not into it. I'm really sorry. I'll just get my things and go."

The woman emits a low laugh. "Babe, this is your room. Don't you even remember picking me up at the bar and taking me here?"

"Sorry, Laurie."

"Yeah, it's Lisa."

"Right. Again. So sorry."

Lisa zips her jeans and throws on her shirt. As she grabs her flip-flops at the edge of the bed, she looks over to Julie who is clearly lost in her own thoughts.

"She really did a number on you."

Julie looks up at Lisa. "Yes, she did."

"I'll let myself out."

Julie hears the hotel door click closed. She leans back against the pillows, stretching her arm across the bed to the empty side. Staring up at the ceiling, she can hear traffic noise outside her window but she longs for the sound of the ocean surf or crickets or something natural and not man-made. As she stretches her legs out farther, she feels something in the bed with her. She reaches down and feels the vibrator Lisa left behind. This is how she knows she's out of it. She had no idea the woman was even using a vibrator on her at all. She turns it on and presses it between her legs. Closing her eyes, she lets the pulsing pull her in and take her away from the present moment. She sees Kat's face before her, smiling. She feels Kat's warm breath on her neck. As her orgasm builds, she whispers aloud to the empty hotel room, "Kat, this is for you. All of my love, all of it is here for you. Take it from me. Please take it. Wherever you are, feel this love from me. Feel it. Please, Kat."

Julie cries out as the orgasm fiercely rocks her body. She lies there, totally spent, with tears streaming down her face.

Kat is wide-awake in bed. She stares at the clock, watching it turn from 3:35 a.m. to 3:36 a.m. Giving up on sleep altogether, she goes into her closet, pulling out an old shoebox from the farthest corner with the word "Memories" written in black magic marker. She sits on the floor of her closet with only the single bulb from the light above. Inhaling deeply, she opens the box. The first photo on top is of her and Molly smiling in front of Molly's house. Kat remembers how hot it was that day, how the dust filled her lungs and made her want to choke.

She sets it aside and rummages through the box looking for one photo in particular. Almost at the bottom, underneath her first number-eight basketball pinnie, she finds what she is looking for: a photo of her mom and dad when her mom was very pregnant with her. Her dad wears bell-bottom jeans and a white T-shirt and sports a thick handlebar mustache. His arm is wrapped possessively around her mom, as if he's showing her off to whoever is taking the photo. In him, she sees so much of her physical attributes. Her dad was tall, at least six feet. He had dark black hair like her, and she notices for the first time that they have the same elbows. It's a weird thing to notice for the first time, but it's true. The same exact elbows. She wonders what he was like as a person, what he loved, what he feared, and what else they have in common.

She turns her attention to her mom. She can tell by the way her eyes look that her mom is sober. The one true gift her mother gave her was remaining sober for the length of her pregnancy. They look happy in the picture. Laughing and full of life.

For years, Kat felt guilty for the intense relief she experienced after her mother's death. Life was so hard with her mom and although she tried to provide for both of them, Kat was just a child forced into becoming an adult way before her time. Every day she worried that her mother would have an accident, or worse yet, would hurt some innocent person. But after Molly's dad came to the house that night, her first instinctive emotion was relief. Relief that it was finally over. Relief that she no longer had to take care of them both.

Kat rises from the closet deciding that a walk on the beach is in order. Cooper sleeps so soundly she decides against disturbing her, slipping quietly out the back door alone.

Kat walks down the stairs to the beach and is surprised how bright the night is with the full moon. Julie is on her mind, more powerfully than usual. She wants so much to contact her, to reach out and tell her how much she misses her. She needs her and the idea of needing anyone is incredibly uncomfortable. Twice, she pulls her cell phone out of her pocket and starts typing a text to her. But what would she say really? What can be said in a text that would say it all? And honestly, judging from the way Julie has been playing of late, Kat is perfectly aware of the anger Julie harbors. She stuffs the phone back in her pocket and keeps walking.

She closes her eyes and is immediately transported back to the night at the bar when they kissed for the first time. Even the memory gives her butterflies. She walks the expansive beach like a ghost in a dream, remembering only what she wants to forget. Julie's face. Her eyes. Her mouth. She imagines looking into those eyes and feeling the warmth crawl up her spine when Julie touches her. Every fiber of her being wants to reach out to Julie. The ache within her comes from a place so deep she can't reach in to make it stop.

Alone. Why do I always feel so alone? She loves Julie. True love. The kind of love you wait a lifetime for. This is the lightning bolt kind of love she and Molly always talked about. This is the real deal, for the rest of her life kind of love and she knows it but everyone she's ever loved has left her. Her father. Her mother. Danielle. Leaving Julie first was just a preemptive strike at the tail end of a long line of heartbreaks.

She can pretend she did it for Julie's career, but with a heavy sigh, she acknowledges that deep down that wasn't the case at all. She did it to protect herself. She just couldn't bear pulling the pieces of herself back together again. Unfortunately, she didn't realize the heartbreak of walking away from Julie on her own terms would be just as gut-wrenching. Never could she have anticipated that her love for Julie would stay with her in every moment, even as she tried to build a new life away from her. *Come to me. Find me. I'm so sorry for leaving you.* Her thoughts of Julie, her memories of her mother and of her childhood tug at her, pull her into a place so deep it makes her tremble with fear, longing, and sadness.

Kat kneels in the sand, letting the water lap up against her legs. She leans back and lets herself feel all of it—every emotion she's locked away all her life. There is something magical about the ocean on this night. For the first time, she feels connected to something greater than herself. For the first time, she feels something akin to faith or God or a universal presence that resides inside every person. The tide pulls her in, holding her as if in an embrace, and then pulls out all of the hurt and sadness, dragging it all away into the endless darkness.

All the pain her mother caused. The sadness of a little girl watching her daddy walk away and never look back. The heartbreak she saw in Julie when she walked away. The past she's run from comes sweeping back like an old broken record. She weeps with a violence that shakes her to her core and something inside of her snaps like a small twig underfoot. She lets the waves roll over her legs and pull every ounce of doubt and pain from her. *Take it all. Take it away. Please. I'm so tired.* She lets the photo of her parents fall from her hands and she watches as the outgoing tide pulls it farther and farther away. For the first time in her life, she lets herself become completely and utterly unhinged.

"Mama, I'm so sorry. I'm so sorry I didn't do better for you," Kat says to the ocean. She feels her mother there, looking down on her. She wonders if her mother knew the relief Kat felt when she died. She wonders if her mother would be proud of her and the life she has created. She asks her for the forgiveness she knows she can only grant herself.

Kat loses all track of time and space, but at some point, she registers the pink and yellow of the coming sunrise as it breaks the horizon. A single gull flies high in the sky, dancing in the wind. She rises, empty and exhausted, shaking the sand from her legs and putting one foot in front of the other as she returns home to start another day.

Chapter Twenty-two

Kat stares out the gallery window rather than focusing on the emails on her computer screen. She just can't seem to pull herself together after last night's breakdown. Yes, it was definitely a breakdown. Admitting it is difficult and unsettling. Kat doesn't normally allow herself to cave in to weakness, and yet she did so last night. She closes out of the email and props her feet up on the desk, sipping her coffee and checking to see if her iPhone, now submerged in a Ziploc baggie full of rice, survived the night's events any better than she did. She turns her cell phone on and is surprised to see it's working just fine. The magic of rice! Moments later, she's dialing a phone number. She needs a cure for what ails her and she knows just the call to make.

"Well, what the hell took you so long?" says the voice on the other end of the line.

"So, I was wondering if you could take a few days off and maybe get some tan on those Irish freckles."

"You know, I have been waiting for this call," Molly says.

"I know. I've been a bad friend."

"You can make it up to me with frosty drinks and hot women."

"Ha. You're on. When can you get here?" Kat asks.

"I'll be there on Monday. Does that work? I have a bunch of comp time I can take."

"Yes! What about Joanne?"

"Nah, I need a few days away from her. We've been driving each other crazy the past few weeks."

"Oh, Molly. I miss you."

"Ditto, babe."

Kat hangs up and looks around the gallery, relieved that Molly is coming for a visit. Molly always knows what to say to make her feel better. She tips her head back and closes her eyes. Suddenly, Abby bursts into the gallery carrying rolls of heavy photographic paper. Kat jumps up to help her.

"Jesus, is this what I pay you for? To keep your feet up on the desk and nap?"

"Oh, Abby, I'm so sorry." Kat swallows. "I was just taking a moment to gather myself. It was a long night."

"Hot date?"

"Hardly. Sleepless night walking the beach and thinking."

"Oh, those are the worst. I've got two more loads in the car. Can you help me get everything in?"

"Sure thing." Kat rushes outside and helps Abby empty her car of supplies for the photo printers and custom framing.

Once the two of them unload and unpack everything, Abby sits behind the desk with Kat, stroking Cooper's head as the dog stares up adoringly at her.

"I have grown to love this dog, I really have."

"Clearly the feelings are mutual. I don't think she's ever looked at me that way."

"What can I say, I have a way with dogs and women."

Kat grins and rolls her eyes.

"So all this nighttime thinking, is this becoming a common occurrence? Because I have a line of equally hot women willing to work in this gallery if you're not up to it." Abby winks, letting Kat know she isn't really serious.

"I hope it isn't becoming common. I can't handle too many nights like that. Last night was really strange for me. It was like something inside me shattered and all these intense emotions of everything I ever held back just came rushing out. I wasn't expecting it. Not after the perfectly lovely evening I had with Antonia. We had dinner at Napi's, and I guess it was a date of sorts, although I don't think she's in town much longer anyway."

"Well, that's why everything came rushing out. Jesus, Kat, you really aren't that tough to figure out, you know."

"What do you mean?"

"Well, here you are on a date with a new woman, a nice woman by all accounts, and you are starting to move on. Your head is telling you one thing and your heart is telling you another. Which one are you going to listen to? That's the real question."

"Who the hell are you and what have you done with my crotchety boss? Since when did you become the Provincetown Love Guru?"

"Listen, babe. Beneath this tough exterior lies a very sensitive soul. I've been around the block more times than I will ever admit, but I'll kill you myself if you tell anyone my secret!"

"Ahh, why is everything so damned complicated?" Kat sighs.

"Because we make it complicated. Now get your ass back to work. I'm not paying you to sit here for these therapy sessions."

"Yes, ma'am. Oh, before I forget, my best friend

Molly is coming to visit next week. Any chance I can maybe take a day or two off?"

"Sure. Clear your schedule with Joyce. If she can handle it, that's fine. I'm going to be off to Nantucket for a couple of photo shoots so I won't be around at all to cover either. Just make sure the money gets deposited in the bank each day. I don't like keeping too much cash on hand when things are this busy. Oh, and we are closed Thursday for Carnival. No point in staying open with all the drunken craziness, which I will also go out of my way to avoid, so enjoy."

"Got it," replies Kat.

෪෫෪෫

Several hours later, Kat takes a moment to down a bottle of water after a particularly hectic day so far. Visitors to the gallery have been coming in nonstop and she hasn't even had a chance to breathe, let alone eat lunch. She can feel her stomach growling and knows she needs to eat soon.

Kat turns to see a woman standing with her back to Kat, staring at a large print of Race Point. The woman's white blond hair is cut short, and she's about five feet eight. Kat's mouth suddenly goes dry and her stomach starts doing flips. She stands frozen in place. It can't be. Is it her? Before she can stop herself, she hears her own voice say, "Julie? Is that you?"

The young woman turns around smiling. "Excuse me?"

Kat blinks back tears. "Oh, sorry. I thought you were someone else."

The woman smiles at Kat. "No problem. I get that a lot."

Kat braces the corner of the desk, holding herself up. Her body's reaction to the possibility that that person was Julie unnerves her. She tries to steady herself, taking deep breath after deep breath until she can feel her pounding heart slow to a manageable pace.

"You look like you have very low blood sugar!" A chipper, cheerful voice knocks Kat out of her foggy state.

Kat blinks back the anxiety to see Antonia smiling at her, holding a bag in front of Kat's face. Something wonderful and delicious is in the bag because with one whiff Kat's stomach begins to growl in earnest.

"Wow. Hi," says Kat, pulling herself together, eying the bag of food like a hungry lion.

"Hi. I thought you could use some lunch. I had no idea what you liked really, but I was walking the pier by the Aqua Bar and got you a veggie burrito at Big Daddy's. That place is always hopping so I figure they make good stuff. I had their tofu, squash, and corn tacos which were awesome."

"How on earth did you know that's my favorite place to get lunch?" Kat beams, truly touched by the gift.

"They are great, aren't they? Call it a hunch."

In no time, Kat's mouth fills with the savory taste of the best burrito in P-Town. In between bites she quips, "Well, it was a good hunch. Sit down with me." She pats the seat next to her.

They sit behind the desk in the shop. Antonia smiles, visibly amused at the sheer speed in which Kat inhales the food. If Kat wasn't so famished, she'd be eying Antonia's legs in her short cutoffs.

"You know, you really should chew the food before you swallow it."

"Please, if you didn't come in when you did, I might've chewed Cooper's leg off."

At the sound of her name plus the smell of food, Cooper rests a paw on Kat's lap, drooling the entire time as she watches Kat finish off the burrito. Kat tosses a piece of tortilla in the air, which Cooper snaps up immediately.

"Busy day today?"

"Crazy busy. It just slowed down a few minutes ago. How are you doing? How's the writing?"

"It's okay. I got a few pages done. I am planning to go back now and write for the rest of the afternoon." Antonia picks at some imaginary lint on her shorts. "This is a little awkward for me. I'm not used to, well, being this forward with someone. Tonight is my last night here before I go back to Cleveland and I was wondering if we could spend it together. I know it sounds crazy and I'm really not the kind of person into one-night stands or anything. I've actually never had a one-night stand. Not that I think this would really be a one-night stand technically since we've been out before but…"

"Antonia, you're rambling again." Kat's shoulders shake with laughter.

Antonia is blushing so hard her cheeks turn nearly purple. Kat laughs again, amused by her discomfort. She rests her hand on Antonia's hand, gently stopping the imaginary lint picking.

"I would love to spend the evening with you. Why don't you come over for dinner? I'll cook. Let's say seven-thirty this evening, okay?"

Antonia looks up at Kat, holding her gaze intently. "Yes, that would be great, but we could go out too if you want."

"No, really I love to cook. It will be my pleasure."

Kat still has her hand on Antonia's. She curls her

fingers around Antonia's, who curls her fingers tighter in return.

"What can I bring?" Antonia asks.

"How about you bring a contribution of wine?"

"Okay, sure."

Antonia leans forward slowly, surprising Kat with an incredibly soft and supple kiss. It's gentle and warm, calming almost.

Kat pulls back first to see Antonia's long eyelashes still closed. She opens her eyes, focusing intently on Kat's then rises quickly, making her way out the door.

"Well, that settles it"—Antonia says as she turns back toward Kat—"I'm definitely not getting any writing done this afternoon." She shakes her finger in mock protest at Kat as she pivots back toward the door.

"You know just the way you said that is going to make me wonder what you are planning to do with yourself this afternoon," says Kat.

Antonia replies just as the door slams shut, "Wouldn't you like to know!"

"Oh, yes I would," says Kat as she watches Antonia walk away.

Chapter Twenty-three

K at sits with her feet up on her deck railing, sipping a glass of wine, listening to Jack Johnson, and staring out at the wide expanse of beach at dead low tide. She's comfortable in a pair of khaki shorts, a white tank top, and her standby blue button-down shirt that's a personal favorite because it's so worn and soft.

She set the table outside on the deck since it's such a lovely and almost unseasonably cool evening with the sky soft and wispy. Christmas lights twinkle brightly around the deck. The breeze off the water is clear and fragrant. Kat thinks about the kiss with Antonia. It didn't blow her socks off. It wasn't the heat, fire, and passion she felt with Julie, but it was comfortable, solid, even sweet. It actually reminds her of the feeling she once had with Danielle. And just as it was with Danielle, she imagines life with Antonia would be just that: comfortable, solid, and sweet although she's not fooled into thinking there would actually be a life with Antonia. She lives in Cleveland with obvious family issues. No, whatever this is will just be for now, for tonight, and that's absolutely fine with her. It's liberating actually, to think there is no future with Antonia. They can just be in the moment and enjoy it without concern or consideration of what tomorrow will bring.

"I thought you would be busy cooking some crazy-complicated dinner," Antonia says as she strides up the wood plank walkway to Kat's house.

"Well, the chef decided on a simple menu so as to truly enjoy the sunset and the company." Kat can't help but notice how beautiful Antonia's hair looks, rich auburn and wavy against the light sky behind her.

"I come bearing gifts of wine." Antonia holds up two bottles. "I wasn't sure if we'd need red or white so I got one of each."

"That's perfect." Kat stands to take both bottles and gives Antonia a lingering kiss on the lips that Antonia leans into.

"Careful, or we'll never get to dinner."

"Would that be so bad?"

"Are you kidding? I've been cooking for hours! C'mon in and welcome to my humble abode."

Kat's place is small, really small actually, but it's cozy and clean. Everything in it says beach house, laid back, and comfortable, with an edge of funky. The living room and kitchen are divided only by a butcher-block center island that Kat refinished and painted white with four barstools of different colors. In the living room space, there is an old rocking chair, a blue-and-white-striped couch, and a rustic-looking coffee table. The end table is an old lobster pot that Kat covered with a glass top. A small gas fireplace stands in the corner, a television mounted above it. The large windows and sliders face out to the water and the expansive ocean views.

While Kat opens a bottle of wine, Antonia bends down to properly greet Cooper, who is extremely happy to have company, especially someone she knows already.

"It's really charming," she says as she looks around the small space, checking out the books lining the built-in bookshelves.

"Charming is another word for small." Kat smirks. "It is small, but Cooper and I don't need much room. Those bookshelves were there, but they were a mess. Down the hall are two bedrooms. One bedroom doubles as an office and guest room, and the bathroom is right there." She points in the general direction of the hallway.

"Something smells absolutely delicious. What is it?"

"Oh, well, I told you the chef was very busy before you arrived," Kat replies as she hands Antonia a glass of wine. "Please sit, make yourself comfortable." Kat motions outside. "I've got a few appetizers. I'll just bring them out."

She pulls a bowl of fresh homemade guacamole from the fridge and a small platter of shucked oysters.

"Here, let me take that," Antonia says. Her fingers graze Kat's briefly as she lifts the bowl of guacamole from Kat's hands.

"The pita chips are right there. Just grab those and we will be all set."

Kat picks up the wine and holds it under her arm and they make their way back outside.

After lighting the three hurricane lanterns and a few candles in huge glass cases, Kat settles down, facing the water view.

"I don't know how you leave here to go to work every day, Antonia says wistfully while she stares out at the water.

"It is tough," Kat murmurs before turning her focus to the food. "Please eat! Those are Wellfleet oysters. I think they're the best in the world, although it's not like I've tried oysters from all over. The guy at the fish market taught me how to shuck them. But I'm not a pro and am apologizing in advance if you get a piece of shell or two. That's guacamole and those are homemade pita chips."

"Impressive," says Antonia. "I tried my first oysters here. We don't really have them in Cleveland."

"Yeah, I didn't have them in Nebraska either."

"So what was it like growing up in Nebraska?"

"Ahh, the dreaded childhood questions," says Kat in a wry tone.

"Oh, I'm sorry, if you don't want to talk about it..."

"No, no, it's fine. It just wasn't easy. My dad left when I was six and my mom was an addict and alcoholic. I didn't really get a chance to be a kid since I was always taking care of her, working to pay the bills, and going to school. She died when I was seventeen."

"Oh no, Kat, I'm so sorry." Antonia touches Kat's arm gently.

"No, don't be. I've come to terms with it recently to be truthful.

"What did you do after your mom died?"

"I moved in with my best friend Molly. Her parents have become surrogate parents to me. It's too bad you're just going to miss Molly. She's coming to visit Monday. You'd love her. She is a piece of work."

"Please, don't remind me that I'm leaving tomorrow." Antonia's eyes meet Kat's. "So how did you end up becoming a referee in the WNBA?"

"For starters, I played basketball in high school and at Notre Dame. I couldn't really make it as a professional player, so I decided to become an official instead."

"Do you miss it?"

"The reffing? No. Not at all. People don't realize what a demanding job it is with all the travel and the shit we take. No one is paying to see us—they're paying to see the players. We're just part of the backdrop. I do miss being around the game, though. I love it so much and loved being on the floor night after night, but I am surprisingly happy here in Provincetown too in ways I never could have imagined."

"Life takes you to unexpected places. Love brings you home," Antonia replies.

"Huh, that's eloquent."

"Oh, I can't take the credit for it. I read it recently in a book called *Mistletoe Magic* by Melissa McClone.

"I'm not sure love brought me here," says Kat. "I mean, I guess it did, but not in the way you'd think."

"Well, that's a little mysterious and convoluted." Antonia quirks a brow.

"Look, you're the writer. I don't have a way with words. I'm not trying to be mysterious really. I left someone and moved out here. She's a player in the WNBA."

"Why didn't it work out?"

"Because I never really gave it a chance to," Kat says honestly.

"Ah. So you are here, alone in Provincetown, because you left someone you cared about and just needed a change?"

"No, because I was afraid."

"I see."

"Look, I'm not hiding anything from you, Antonia. It's been a rough few months for me with a lot of soul-searching. But I don't want to talk about that. It's too depressing and complicated and this is such a gorgeous night. I want to talk about you. I don't want to waste tonight talking about all our could have's and should have's. Tell me about you," Kat says as she pours them both more wine and pops an oyster into her mouth.

"We couldn't be any more different, really," Antonia manages to say, her mouth full of guacamole. "I mean when it comes to our childhoods. I have two younger brothers. Michael is in the doctoral program at Michigan State studying forensic science, of all things. My other brother, John, lives in Montana teaching fly fishing lessons at a ranch. My parents have been married for over fifty years. My dad tells me all the time that they were both the love of each other's lives. My dad was a music teacher for thirty-five years before he was forced to retire after the music programs were shut down due to budget cuts and my mom was a nurse."

"And your mom has Alzheimer's?" Kat asks.

"Yes. She had early onset about five years ago but it hit really hard and fast. About six months ago we had to move her into a nursing home facility for live-in care. My dad suffered a stroke because he was trying to do everything for both of them."

"And your brothers, do they help?"

Antonia chuckles at the question. "That's a good one. No. They don't help. They both have their heads in the sand regarding our parents. Neither of them lives close by. So that responsibility falls on me. I don't mind, really. As the only girl, I always sort of expected it. I want to do whatever I can for both of them, but..."

"But it's hard to put your life on hold to take care of them," Kat responds.

"Exactly. You know what you said a few minutes ago about not hiding anything? Well, I really like you, Kat. It's been a rough few months for me too. I'm enjoying your company and this chance to get away from my life for a while. I want to make the most of this time and worry about tomorrow when tomorrow comes. You know?"

"Absolutely. And I'm with you one hundred percent. So let's toast." Kat raises her glass and so does Antonia. "To today."

"To today."

"On that note, let me just go inside and get dinner."

"I'll help!"

"No, everything is done. I just need to bring it out. Please, sit here and relax with Cooper. I'll be out in a few. I'm going to change the music. Anything in particular?"

"No preference. Your call," Antonia says.

Kat brings the empty plates and wine bottle into the kitchen. She changes the music to one of her personal favorites, Brandi Carlile, and prepares their dishes. Before Antonia arrived, Kat grilled skirt steak after it marinated for hours in a homemade chimichurri sauce. She made a tabouli salad and mixed in cubed, grilled, farm-local eggplant and zucchini along with parsley, green onion, and lemon zest. Her favorite part of the meal is an heirloom tomato salad loaded with locally made mozzarella cheese, basil, and grilled sweet corn. For good measure, she cut up a baguette so they could dip the bread into the juice from the tomato salad.

One by one, Kat brings out each dish until Antonia sits speechless at the table. When Kat finally sits down herself after opening another bottle of wine, Antonia says, "This is incredible. I don't know what I would do with myself if I had someone as breathtaking as you cooking me meals like this night after night."

Touched by the compliment, Kat leans over and kisses her for a long moment.

"I mean it, Kat, you are stunning." Antonia looks deep into her eyes.

"If you're trying to get me into bed it's working."

"Shit, really? Right now? But everything looks so good! I'd hate to waste this incredible meal."

Kat bursts out into laughter. "Well then, we'd better get busy eating this delicious dinner."

Long after they finish eating, they sit outside talking around the small fire pit on Kat's back deck. The heat and glow from the fire feels cozy and comforting on the slightly cool night. Even Kat is a little surprised at how easy things are with Antonia and how well they seem to mesh. After the table is cleared and the dishes washed, thanks to Antonia, Kat suggests a walk on the beach. Cooper hears the word "beach" and hops up out of a sound sleep.

"We need to take a walk after all that food! If this art gallery gig doesn't work out, you should open a restaurant. People would pay good money to eat the food you cook," says Antonia.

"Oh no, I just do it for fun. The moment cooking becomes a job, I'm sure I'd feel very differently about it." Kat looks up at the full moon, shimmering brightly in the night sky.

"*La Bella Luna*," Antonia says wistfully, looking up at the moon too.

"What's that?" Kat asks.

"La Bella Luna. It means the beautiful moon in Italian. My mom always said it every time she saw the full moon."

Kat reaches for Antonia's hand and they stroll down the beach in a companionable silence. The thought occurs to Kat that her emotions are so different on the beach tonight than they were the other night. The ocean seems to be matching her inner emotions. When her feelings boiled over, the water was unsettled, the waves rocky. But tonight, as she relaxes completely with Antonia, the water is calm and serene.

"What are you thinking?" Antonia asks.

"I am thinking how relaxed I am with you right now," Kat responds.

"Mmm. Me too." Antonia's fingers tighten around Kat's.

"Shall we turn around?" Kat asks, sensing a change in Antonia's demeanor.

"Sure. Yes, I'm getting a little chilly."

Kat calls for Cooper to come back with them. She unbuttons her long-sleeve shirt, revealing a white tank top underneath, and gives it to Antonia. "Here, put this on."

Antonia accepts it gratefully. As she puts it on, she gently smells the collar. "What is the perfume you wear?"

"Calvin Klein's Eternity. Do you like it?

"Very much."

They walk back to the house, neither one speaking. Expectancy hovers in the air between them yet Kat doesn't find it unnerving.

When they reach the top of the deck stairs, Kat opens the door for Cooper to return to the house but Antonia stands back.

"I should go," she says quietly. "It's pretty late."

Kat walks back to her, placing her hands on either side of her face. Very gently she kisses Antonia on the lips. Antonia is tentative at first, but as the kiss deepens, Kat can feel her relax into the kiss. Kat slowly traces the outline of Antonia's lips with her tongue. Sighing, Antonia wraps her arms around Kat's waist.

Kat pulls away from the kiss. "You can go if you want, but I'd rather you stay."

"Who said anything about leaving?" Antonia's eyes sparkle.

Kat laughs, pulling her into the house, kissing her again as the door closes behind them.

Once inside, she leads Antonia down the hallway to her bedroom. The moon is so bright it illuminates the room with a cool blue glow. Antonia caresses Kat's face. "You are so beautiful," she muses, running her fingers down Kat's jawbone to her neck. Kat tips her neck back, making room for Antonia to kiss her there and she obliges. Kat removes Antonia's clothes slowly, taking in her exquisite body in the moonlight. She watches Antonia's breasts rise and fall with every breath and sees her shudder when her fingertips graze her nipples. Antonia sits on the edge of the bed, watching Kat as she takes her own clothes off. She wraps her arms around Kat again, kissing her breasts, her stomach, and her hipbone. Kat straddles Antonia, forcing her to lie down on the bed.

Their lovemaking begins gently and slowly. Antonia is a generous lover, taking every opportunity to caress Kat, to kiss her. Kat doesn't remember feeling this at ease and relaxed with any other lover during their first time.

Rolling Kat onto her back, Antonia moves down Kat's body. Just as Kat expects to spread her legs apart, she hears Antonia hoarsely command, "Turn over."

A little surprised, Kat turns over onto her stomach. Antonia gently moves Kat's long black hair away from her neck so her mouth and tongue can explore her neck, her earlobe. Kat sighs into the pillow, stretching her arms out across the bed, reveling in the feeling of Antonia's body against hers.

Antonia moves down Kat's back, caressing her

shoulders, her back, her sides, her spine with feather-light touches. When she reaches the dimple in the small of Kat's back, Kat can't help but arch up. She feels Antonia's hands cupping her ass, teasing her until she rises up on her knees while her face remains buried in the pillow. She is aching for Antonia to touch her, to taste her.

Antonia doesn't hesitate, burying her face in between Kat's legs from behind. Her fingers deftly pull Kat's hips toward her lips and Kat makes full use of the opportunity, rocking against Antonia's mouth and grinding slowly as Antonia uses her tongue, her teeth, and her mouth to apply firm pressure. Quickly, Antonia shifts gears, sliding three fingers deep inside of Kat, surprising her yet again. Kat continues to rock, this time against Antonia's hand, needing more. Antonia encircles her waist with her other arm and now strokes Kat's clitoris from the front, setting off shudders of pure delight.

Kat allows herself to be pleasured completely by Antonia. She moans with her head still buried in the pillow. The orgasms that come one after the other don't cause her to levitate off the bed, but they are steady and flood her body with warmth. She hears Antonia talking to her, but she doesn't decipher the words because of the buzzing sensation in her brain.

Kat turns over onto her back, pulling Antonia toward her. Unexpectedly, Antonia straddles her face. She begins to rock, slowly and Kat matches her rhythm with her tongue and mouth. Kat laces her fingers into Antonia's on either side. She sucks and flicks Antonia's incredibly swollen clitoris with a methodical pace. Then she slides her tongue as deep into Antonia as she can, over and over again. Antonia shifts, holding onto the wrought iron headboard with both hands, rotating her hips freely, openly and without any hesitation, to match the rhythm and movement of Kat's tongue.

Kat feels the searing intensity of Antonia's muscles contracting and releasing. Suddenly, she is aware how incredibly hot the room has become. Antonia moans, "Oh. My. God. That feels so good." Kat would say the same thing if her mouth wasn't already engaged.

Focusing all of her attention on Antonia's clitoris, she knows she can make her come at any moment. Yet, every time she feels Antonia's body tighten, she moves her tongue away, teasing her, drawing the orgasm out over what feels like an eternity until it's Kat who feels like she is going to explode. Antonia rocks forward, arches her back, and tips her head back as a long, slow low moan escapes her lips. Kat watches Antonia's body, slick with sweat, glimmering in the moonlight and feels her own orgasm building. As Antonia comes, Kat tastes the sweetness of her orgasm as it floods her mouth.

Antonia leans forward into the headboard, breathing hard, her thighs quivering on either side of Kat's face. If it weren't for Kat's arms on her sides, Antonia would probably fall over, which she does after a few moments, panting next to Kat. Antonia gazes at her. "That was—" but before she can finish, Kat rolls on top of her.

"This is what you taste like," Kat says to Antonia, kissing her deeply, their tongues tangling.

Both of them covered with sweat, Antonia slides her hands up and down Kat's body. As they kiss, she rolls Kat over onto her back.

"I need a second," Kat says with a laugh.

"No, you don't," Antonia murmurs as she takes turns sucking and biting Kat's nipples. "I think you're ready to come again. Right now."

"It's okay. I'm okay," is all Kat says before Antonia's mouth finds its mark and Kat decides the contrary. While Antonia's fingers roll over and play with Kat's nipples, her tongue is doing some magical swirling thing that is blowing Kat's mind. For a second, Kat focuses on trying to figure out what Antonia is doing to her, but after a few more of those magical, mystical swirls, Kat's brain ceases working entirely and her body takes control of the wheel.

"I'm not sure what you are doing but please, please don't stop," whispers Kat, as her hands press Antonia's head more firmly into place.

Kat's orgasm hits quickly, surprising her with its sudden ferocity. She cries out and the aftershocks that rock her body make her head swim. Somewhere in the hazy distance, she sees Julie's face looking down on her, smiling. Kat draws in a ragged breath, trying to slow the freight train that is her breathing as Antonia now lies with her head on Kat's stomach.

The two are silent for a few minutes, giving Kat time to gather herself. There is no mistaking that she and Antonia have physical chemistry. Even Kat is surprised at how confident and free Antonia is in bed, as compared to her calm and almost shy demeanor out of it. But she knows the kind of feeling she has for Antonia doesn't come close to matching the soul-clenching, otherworldly emotions she has with Julie. The question is, can this be enough? Would it ever be enough? Who is she kidding? Antonia leaves for Cleveland tomorrow and it's not as if she is going to move there next week. Then again, long-distance relationships can work if both are committed to them.

As these thoughts rattle around in Kat's brain, she

almost doesn't catch the question Antonia asks as she rises up to make eye contact with her.

"Who is Julie?" Antonia asks again, gently brushing away a damp strand of black hair from Kat's face.

At the sound of Julie's name, Kat's emotions ride a tidal surge of sadness, passion, hope, love, and longing and Antonia catches all of them as she looks deeply into Kat's eyes.

"She's the one, isn't she? The player you left to come here?"

Kat doesn't say anything but tries to turn her head away from Antonia's gaze. Antonia doesn't let her, pushing her face back. "Kat, it's okay. Tell me the truth."

"Yes," is all Kat can manage. "But, Antonia, please don't think…"

"It's okay, Kat," Antonia says, kissing her again. "I'm a big girl. I knew from our first dinner that you were still in love with someone else. I could sense it. I don't have any misconceptions that either one of us is going to drop everything to make a relationship work. I'm making no claim on you, but I still wanted this to happen and I still wanted to share the experience with you. In a way, I think we both needed it."

Kat looks deeply into Antonia's eyes, smiling. "You really are an amazing woman, Antonia. I hope someday you find someone who will tell you that every day. You deserve it."

"Damn right I deserve it. But in the meantime, I can always think back to this incredibly hot night with you that I'm pretty sure will get me through some long winter nights in Cleveland."

As Kat pulls the sheet over them both, thinking they will settle into a comfortable sleep, Antonia slips her head underneath the covers, kissing Kat's body all over again.

"You can't be serious," Kat says, once again warming to her touch.

From beneath the covers, Antonia responds, "Hey, I'm making the most out of this one night. Don't think you are going to sleep anytime soon. Consider it research. For my writing."

"Um hmm." Kat chortles.

⚜ ⚜ ⚜ ⚜

Kat wakes slowly from an incredibly deep sleep because the sunlight of the new day is shining squarely in her face. She smells something fragrant. Stretching, she expects to reach out and touch Antonia. But after a few seconds, the thought registers that Antonia is not in bed with her. Kat squints her eyes open to see the clock reading 10:15.

Sitting up in bed, Kat notices a vase of honeysuckle and a note on her nightstand. She stretches out completely, satiated and relaxed from almost seven hours of nonstop lovemaking. Unfolding the note she reads:

Kat:
Thank you for healing me, waking me, seeing me.
"In your light, I learn how to love. In your beauty, how to make poems. You dance inside my chest where no-one sees you, but sometimes I do, and that sight becomes this art." —Rumi

Don't hide from the love you are meant for; have the courage to live it.

Besos,
Antonia
PS: I fed Cooper and took her for a long walk.
Breakfast for you is in the kitchen.

Kat lies back, looking up at the ceiling. She knows
Antonia is gone, headed back to Cleveland, and it occurs
to her that she has no idea how to reach her. No phone
number, no last name. Just Antonia from Cleveland who
found a way to give her back a broken piece of her heart.

Chapter Twenty-four

Two days after Antonia's departure, Kat sits once again on the back deck looking out at the water and drinking a glass of wine. This time, she's waiting for someone else to walk up the steps. She smiles as soon as she hears the car door slam shut before she even hears her best friend's voice.

"Where is my home girl at?" yells Molly as she bounds up the stairs.

"Why do you insist on talking all ethnic when you are the whitest person I know?" Kat squeezes her friend tightly in a bear hug.

"Breathe. I need to breathe," Molly says, wheezing.

Kat releases her and Molly takes a good look around. "Wow. I can see why you packed up life in New York to come out here. This is beautiful, babe. First things first. Where is the dog?"

"Cooper! Come!" Cooper comes bounding up the stairs and immediately greets Molly. Molly sits down on the deck, loving Cooper up. She pulls a squeak toy from her bag, handing it to Cooper who immediately takes off down the stairs to the beach, squeaking wildly. "I honestly can't believe you have a dog. She's very sweet. You got lucky. Some lab-pit mixes are nuts."

"I know. She is the sweetest thing ever. Come in. Let me give you the ten-second tour."

Kat shows Molly her little house, dropping her bags in the back bedroom. After Molly settles in, the two enjoy a quick lunch comprised of cold beer and a tomato-and-avocado sandwich. They decide to spend the rest of the afternoon at Race Point since it's an ideal beach day.

After they pack up the car with chairs, a small umbrella, and a cooler filled with beer, they say goodbye to a sleepy Cooper and head off a few short miles down Route 6 toward Race Point.

"Now these are the days I try to conjure up when it's seven below zero, dark, and snowing," muses Molly a few minutes later as she lies in a reclining beach chair with her eyes closed to the sun.

"Mmm," Kat says as she stretches out on her own beach chair.

"Okay. Let's get down to business. First, what are we doing this weekend? Second, toss me one of those Coronas, please. And third, why do I get the sense your vagina is open for business again?"

Kat bursts out laughing at the last remark. "Okay, first, this is Carnival week. Town will be inundated. I've got today and tomorrow off, but I have to work Wednesday, so you will be left to your own devices. Thursday, the gallery is closed so we are catching the parade. It goes right by the house. I hear it's totally nuts. Second, here is your Corona. And third, how on earth did you know that?"

"It's a vibration thing," Molly says, dead serious.

"What?"

"A vibration thing. I have like a lesbian tuning fork or something. I can always tell when someone just got laid, and you, my sweet best friend, definitely just got laid. So spill the beans and fill me in, pronto. Before I get heat stroke and pass out."

"Well, it's a long story," Kat says.

"Do you see me going anywhere anytime soon? Spill it."

Kat proceeds to fill Molly in on the details of her time with Antonia. She even tries as best she can to explain her little breakdown incident on the beach. Kat talks as they take a dip in the still cold ocean and settle back into their beach chairs, shifting their positions like sundials in the late afternoon sun.

"So you have no idea how to reach this Antonia if you wanted to reconnect with her?" Molly asks finally.

"Not really. I mean I guess I could ask the inn for her contact information. I'm sure they would give it to me. Why, you think I should call her?"

"No, I'm not saying that. I'm just surprised you let her go that easily."

"Well, it was kind of this free-flowing thing we had. It's hard to explain. I'm not sure we would survive a real relationship, but within the confines of a week-long vacation, it was nearly perfect."

Molly brushes some sand off her legs and looks hard at Kat.

"Kat, I see how beautiful it is here and you seem more relaxed and at ease than I think I might ever remember you being, but you are all alone out here. And by out here, I mean edge of the earth, removed from everyone and everything. Do you really want to be this isolated? Not to mention away from basketball? Mom and Dad are worried sick about you. To be honest, so am I."

Kat peers out at the water, trying to find the right words to explain why she is here. She sighs deeply before she speaks. "Molly, I love her. My heart aches for her. I think about her a million times a day. It might be a song lyric or the way the sunset looks. I dream about her. Even the smallest details of my days and nights somehow remind me of her."

She continues, "but my reasons for walking away from her changed, as I have taken the time to really understand myself. I told her and I told myself I was walking away from her to protect her career, but in truth, I was trying to protect myself from getting hurt again. The only way I figured that out was to detach completely and come here. This place has healed me in a lot of ways, and for the first time in my life, I'm not pushing toward a career or a status. That's why I'm so relaxed. I'm just trying to be the best me I can be, and it just so happens to be in this magical place at the edge of the earth as you say."

"And is your plan to stay out here?"

"Honestly, I don't know. I'm trying not to look too far down the road. Would it be so bad if I did stay out here?"

"Well, it would be a problem, I mean how would you help me pick a dress and plan a wedding?" Molly smirks.

"What? Wait. When?"

"Joanne finally popped the question a few weeks ago. I wanted to tell you in person so unknit those eyebrows, please. We are getting married in April, and of course, I want you to be my maid of honor. You know I can't manage all these details without you!"

"Oh my God, Molly, I am so excited for you! Wait, how did Joanne propose? This I need to hear."

"Ha. She took me away to a little cabin up by Saranac Lake. She made me wait outside for like ten minutes. That really bugged me because I had to pee so badly." Kat snorts. "What?" Molly says innocently. "It was a long ride," she continues. "Anyway, she called me on my cell phone and told me to meet her upstairs. I had no idea what she was doing. So, I went inside and as I climbed the stairs leading to the bedroom, I discovered she'd had all these pictures of us blown up on big canvases and had hung them on the wall. In between the pictures were the words 'will you marry me,' but they appeared as separate words all along the way. When I got to the top, she was down on one knee waiting for me with the ring in her hand."

Kat takes a second to close her gaping mouth. "Molly, I can't believe it."

"I know! Who knew Joanne had it in her? I was so shocked and surprised at how much thought she put into it. Ahh...I have been dying to tell you all of this."

Kat cracks open two more Coronas and hands one to Molly. "This we definitely need to toast. To you and Joanne. I'm so happy for you both."

"Cheers."

Both women take a long swig of ice-cold beer. "I just can't get over Joanne," laughs Kat.

"Tell me about it. The sex we had that night was epic too. Her romantic gesture totally livened things up. And she brought toys, so that didn't hurt."

"Who knew Joanne was into toys?"

"Oh, you have no idea. So now you know why I need you back home with me."

"Well, whether I am here or not, we will figure it out. I'll be the best maid of honor I can be."

"Pinky swear?"

"Pinky swear," says Kat.

"And, are we inviting you plus one?"

"It's a little early to be asking me that, isn't it?"

"What, I'm curious. Are you planning to reach out to Julie at some point and work all of this out?"

"How on earth am I going to contact her? Do you honestly think she'd take a call from me or read a text? From the looks of the way she's been annihilating opponents, I think that woman is harboring some deep-seated anger and resentment toward me," Kat says as she picks the label off the Corona bottle.

"Do you blame her? I mean you did crush her heart into a million little bits by saying sayonara after connecting the way you did with her."

"No, I don't blame her at all. I totally understand it. But I think things are the way they are for a reason."

"Yeah, it's called your stubborn streak."

"Hey, I'm not stubborn, I'm right!"

"Oh, please. I know everything about you and I have an impeccable memory," Molly says dramatically.

"Don't start quoting *Beaches*. Once we start, we won't be able to stop," Kat responds.

"I know. You're right. God, I love that movie." Molly chuckles. "*Beaches* is so us."

"Yeah, except you're not Bette Midler and I don't have a wonky heart. But other than that, it's us all right."

Kat grabs Molly's hand. "I'm so glad you're here. I've missed you."

"Ditto, babe. Ditto to that."

Chapter Twenty-five

Neither Kat nor Molly has ever experienced Carnival and all its glory, and to their delight, Kat's house is at the beginning of the parade route. They set up an elaborate mini-party for two outside Kat's house on Thursday morning complete with beach chairs, umbrellas, a cooler, bags of Mardi Gras rainbow-colored beads, and rainbow flags. At one-thirty, they bring out three large pitchers of margaritas gently stashed in the cooler filled with ice. All the neighbors are basically doing the same thing, making for a several-mile-long giant block party.

Even though Provincetown is a tiny place at the tip of Cape Cod, it packs a giant punch for the Carnival parade. Tens of thousands of people come from all over the country to enjoy the first and longest running festival of its kind in all of New England. This year's theme is "Jungle Fantasy," so Kat and Molly oblige by wearing leopard print tank tops painted with giant peace signs, daisy duke jean shorts, and vinyl go-go boots they picked up at the crazy marine supply store that always has something for everyone.

They sit in their beach chairs sipping on margaritas. "This is freaking awesome!" says Molly as she peers up the road to see the parade starting to move.

A town crier passes by the house dressed up as a pilgrim yelling, "Hear ye, hear ye, all is well in Provincetown," marking the official start of the parade.

Five minutes later, the moving party is in full swing. It's a hot, sunny day and the parade participants are already glistening with sweat but no one seems to care. Pulsing floats with gorgeous dancing men pass by. Then come the dykes on bikes wearing their black leather and rainbow flags. Hot women, hot men, and everything in between laugh, dance, and party their way down Commercial Street to the end of the parade at the Boatslip Beach Club.

Kat is amazed at the costumes, the colors, and the sheer volume of gorgeous drag queens wearing impossibly high heels and elaborate makeup with tremendous grace. It is a veritable feast of eye candy. "Put your paws up!" yell hot men as a float passes by with Lady Gaga's "Born this Way" blaring on megaspeakers.

Before they know it, Kat and Molly are dancing in the street with men, with women, tossing their beads to dancing people on floats, sharing their margaritas with anyone who has a cup.

An hour later, they watch the last very drunk parade straggler stagger by. They close up shop at home and make sure Cooper is comfortable in the air conditioning before following the end of the parade into town.

Once they hit the mountain of people on Commercial Street, they finally understand what all the fuss is about. The parade was just foreplay. The real party is happening in the center of town. It truly is just like Mardi Gras in New Orleans. People hang out windows of upstairs apartments, singing and tossing beads. Everyone is drinking or drunk, and everyone with a pulse is dancing, making out, or feeling someone up. It's loud, irreverent, and raucous. Molly and Kat are swept up into the mayhem, grabbing hands to make sure they don't lose each other in the throngs of people. No one cares how hot it is. Every now and then, people run to the water just to cool off and return to the street to dance some more.

Both loaded, the two dance and laugh their way through Commercial Street as people spray them with garden hoses. This is the most fun Kat has had maybe ever. At one point, she turns to see Molly giving her a thumbs-up sign while making out with some gorgeous blond woman.

Four hours later, Kat and Molly stagger back up the stairs to Kat's house. Their heat hangovers have already set in and they are exhausted beyond belief.

"This has been one of the best days. Ever." Molly sighs as she sprawls across Kat's couch with a bag of frozen peas on her forehead.

"Ever," Kat seconds her. She is spread-eagle on the floor with her eyes closed. She starts laughing as Cooper licks her sweaty face.

"What's so funny?"

"Are you going to tell your fiancée you made out with some hot blonde?"

"Did I really? Jesus, I don't even remember that. What a shame. How hot was she?"

"Hot."

"What happens in Provincetown stays in Provincetown," declares Molly, pointing a wobbly finger skyward.

"Deal." Kat grins. "I don't want you to leave tomorrow."

"Me neither."

"I'm starving, but too tired to make anything," Kat says, groaning.

They both sit up at the same time. "Pizza!" they yell in unison, falling back down laughing.

Chapter Twenty-six

Julie closes her eyes, trying to ignore the searing discomfort of sitting stomach-deep in an ice-bucket whirlpool. It's mid-September and she is burned out both mentally and physically. Her hip flexors are inflamed, or so Melanie the trainer tells her, hence the ice-bucket whirlpool after every game and practice. The first five to seven minutes are the most uncomfortable, but after a while, the ice-cold, swirling water actually begins to feel warm. It's an odd bodily phenomenon that Julie is grateful for right about now.

Her New York Liberty team must win tomorrow or their season is over. The Conference Semifinals are comprised of an incredibly short three-game series. Once again, Julie finds herself battling against Connecticut. Both teams won a game, so tomorrow's third and deciding game matters. Win or go home, as they say. Julie knows her team is relying on her to make big shots consistently. Her high level of play from the all-star break on is what has helped propel New York to this point.

As much as Julie wants to win, she is admittedly tired. Her body is bruised from neck to calf and her mind is weary. As she leans her head back against the rolled towel behind her in the stainless steel tub, she closes her eyes and thinks about a deserted expanse of beach and how lovely it would be just to be alone and hear the ocean waves rolling against the shore.

An egg timer rings next to her. "Okay, Stevens. Time's up. You can hop out," says Melanie, knocking her out of her reverie. Melanie helps Julie climb out of the whirlpool and hands her a couple of towels to dry off. "Make sure you come in early tomorrow. I want to be sure we massage you well to loosen you up before pregame," Melanie says.

"Sure thing. Thanks, Melanie. See you tomorrow," Julie replies, heading for the locker room and a hot shower.

Twenty minutes later, Julie is sitting alone in the locker room, getting dressed to go home when she sees her phone vibrating on her locker shelf. She quickly glances at the caller ID, which only reads "Unknown Caller."

"Hello?"

"Hi. Is this Julie Stevens?" the female voice on the other end of the line asks.

"It is. Who's this?"

"My name is Molly."

"Molly? Sorry, I don't know a Molly. So..." Julie says, a little annoyed, as she prepares to hang up.

"No, wait. Don't hang up. I'm a friend of Kat's. Kat Schaefer."

At the sound of Kat's name, every muscle in Julie's body tenses up, and she freezes, unable to speak.

"Hello? Julie? Are you still there?" asks Molly after a few moments.

"Sorry, yes, I'm still here. What is it you want?" asks Julie tersely.

"Would it be possible to meet up? I'd really like to talk with you."

"Um, I don't think that's possible. I don't really have anything to say and I'm busy."

"Look, please, it's important. You're probably in Tarrytown, right, at the Madison Square Garden training facility? I'm not too far away. We could meet up for coffee. How about Coffee Lab Roasters on Main Street? Do you have a car?" Molly rushes out the barrage of questions before Julie has a chance to hang up.

"Um, yeah, I have a car. I'm just finishing up here. I guess I could be there in about twenty minutes."

"Okay great! See you then."

Julie puts the phone down and slumps on the bench in front of her locker. This was not a call she was expecting. Her mind travels back to the time she walked around Kat's house after they made love for the first time. She remembers seeing photos of Kat and Molly as kids. She remembers the phone ringing and Kat saying, "It's my best friend Molly." She remembers feeling so utterly content in that moment with Kat.

She snaps herself back to the present and proceeds to tie her sneakers. She grabs her bag and heads for the door, wondering if something happened to Kat.

❧❧❧❧

Thirty minutes later, Julie enters the coffee shop to see a pretty redhead wearing blue scrubs waving in her direction. She cautiously approaches the table.

"Hi, Julie. I'm Molly. Thanks for meeting me. I got you a cappuccino. Hope that's okay."

Julie sits down at the table. "Sure, that's great. Thanks. You a nurse?"

"No, I'm a vet tech." Molly stirs her coffee and an awkward silence ensues.

"So, Molly, why are you here? If Kat sent you to say something or whatever that's really low of her."

Molly sits back in her chair, looking intently at Julie. "No, Julie. Kat has absolutely no idea I am here with you. In fact, I have no doubt that if she knew she'd kill me."

"Then, how did you get my number?" Julie asks, confused.

"I was visiting Kat recently and I stole her cell phone for a few minutes to get it. She really has no idea."

"Visiting Kat? Don't you guys live near each other? You make it sound like she's in another country or something," Julie says a little more sarcastically than she intended.

"She does, in a way." Molly smiles, trying desperately to break through Julie's tough exterior. "She moved to Provincetown, you know, way out on Cape Cod? She's been living there since the spring.

Julie's mind whirls. The beach. All she can think of is that freaking expanse of beach, Kat's eyes, and her smile. "So what? Why are you even telling me this?"

"I thought I would tell you where she was, well, in case you wanted to see her."

Julie is angry. Really angry. "See her?" Are you kidding me? Do you know what she did to me? She left me. She left after what I thought was the beginning of something pretty amazing. She gave me some stupid excuse about my career and then she vanished into thin air. You don't think I tried to call her? Text her? I wrote her letters even. Letters! Who even actually writes letters anymore? I tried for two months until I finally got the picture. And now, you want me to what? Just leave my team in the middle of Conference Semifinals to go surprise her in Provincetown?" Julie rises from the table. "I've got to go. I don't have time for this bullshit."

Molly expected a little pushback from Julie, but

she definitely didn't expect this fire and anger. Clearly, Kat hurt her far more than she even let on. Molly can't help but notice how beautiful Julie is even in the middle of an anger meltdown.

"Julie, please, sit down." Molly's voice takes on a pleading tone.

Julie slumps back down in the chair, shredding the napkin in front of her.

Molly continues, softly, "Look, Julie, I'm here for Kat. She misses you, but she's too stubborn to admit that to you."

Julie cuts in before Molly continues. "Misses me? She walked away from me! I hope she hurts. I hope she feels an ounce of the pain I have felt this past year."

"She loves you," Molly says simply.

Julie stares at Molly, her emotions surging and bubbling to the surface. "I can't do this right now. I can't. I have to focus. I have the biggest game of my life tomorrow. I just can't...handle...this right now." Julie's voice trembles as she fights back tears.

Molly slides a piece of paper across the table to her. "Here is her address. In case. In case you decide to see her."

Julie stares at the address. 552 Commercial Street Provincetown. Her tears slam onto the table. She leaves the paper on the table and heads for the door without another look in Molly's direction.

Chapter Twenty-seven

Kat sits down on the couch with a bowl of popcorn and a beer. She flips her television on, tuning into ESPN2. She pats the couch next to her so Cooper can climb up and snuggle next to her. Her little gas fireplace is putting out just enough heat to warm up the room on the chilly and windy September afternoon.

Dorothy Hall, one of the best basketball announcers in the business, is talking about Julie. "No doubt, New York will get a lift from the home crowd, but they will need Julie Stevens to play a superstar caliber game if they're going to pull off the win against a strong Connecticut team," Hall says.

Kat munches on the popcorn, sharing it almost kernel by kernel with Cooper. She tries to stuff away the pang of anxiety for Julie, the butterflies at the sight of her, and the twinge of jealousy for not being there in person to feel the energy of the game on the court.

The game starts slowly, both teams feeling each other out and feeling the refs out to see how the game will be called. Kat sees Deb, Marcus, and Dave calling the game. That's a great crew, she thinks. She knows the game will be called well and fairly.

Julie starts slow too, missing her first three jumpers. Kat notices something different in her demeanor on the court. She's been following Julie's play all season and she's become accustomed to watching Julie perform with a wild ferocity, but that intensity seems to be missing so far today.

"C'mon, Julie. Step into gear. Don't force the game. Let it come to you," Kat finds herself talking to the television.

As if on cue, Dorothy Hall makes a similar observation. "I know Stevens has been bothered with a nagging hip flexor injury, but she's definitely having a slow start here today, one that the Liberty cannot afford."

The first half is slow and not terribly entertaining to watch. Julie finishes the lackluster half with only six points and two rebounds. The Connecticut Sun lead the New York Liberty 36–29.

Something is up with her, thinks Kat. Something is different. Something is wrong.

During the half, Kat takes Cooper to the beach for a quick run with the Frisbee. She muses about what must be going on in the locker room. Is Julie having problems with teammates? That doesn't seem likely. Maybe she's more severely injured than she's letting on. Kat tries to think through all the possibilities while she plays with Cooper. Her internal clock knows exactly how long it takes for the second half to kick off. Sure enough, she plops back down on the couch with Cooper just as play resumes.

Julie starts out the second half acting more like herself. The fire seems to be back as she hits two quick jumpers just inside the three-point line. Her team senses the energy shift, combining to play solid defense and scooping up the rebounds from the Sun's misses. In a few minutes, Connecticut calls a quick thirty-second timeout to stem the tide from New York. With the score now 36–33, Connecticut is clinging to a three-point lead but the momentum is all New York's.

Kat watches Julie work on offense. She is tireless, constantly moving, constantly changing speeds and directions in order to free herself along the baseline or the perimeter. Connecticut tries to double her whenever she touches the ball near the paint, but Julie sees it coming and dishes the ball to teammates for easy layups or wide open jumpers. With six minutes remaining, it's either team's game for the taking as the lead flips from one team to the other on nearly every possession.

Kat feels relieved to see Julie back in command of the game. She pats Cooper on the head, keeping an eye on the clock and the score.

Suddenly, Kat sees Julie go sprawling after an elbow to the face as she tries to make a backdoor cut to the basket. Deb blows the whistle, convening the refs near the scorer's table to review the call. It happened so fast, Kat didn't get a good look at it so she waits for the replay. Kat knows full well the discussion by the officiating crew is whether or not the hit to Julie is intentional. The Garden sound system plays the Jeopardy theme song since the officials are taking a long while to determine their ruling. Julie is helped off the court, her nose bleeding badly.

While the crew cleans the blood off the floor and the trainer tends to Julie's face, Kat strains to see Julie up close, to see for herself how badly she is hurt. She watches the replay too. It's clear that the contact is not intentional. Julie just caught an inadvertent, albeit extremely hard, elbow. After a few moments, Dorothy Hall makes sense of the call. She says, "A personal foul on Connecticut's Amber Holt has been called, but the officials did not call an intentional foul. I think that's the right call. She hit Stevens hard, don't get me wrong, but she didn't do it intentionally. The clock has been reset to five minutes, forty-five seconds." The New York crowd boos the call and Julie is absolutely seething on the sideline with a gauze pad shoved up her nose.

Liberty Coach Moira Clery keeps Stevens on the sideline for only seventeen seconds before inserting her back into the game. Kat can see it written all over Julie's face. She is out for blood. Control yourself, Julie. Control your anger, she thinks. But Julie seems to be past that. That hit mentally took Julie Stevens out of the game. Every jumper she misses, she complains to the officials that she's being hit on the arm. She is called for two quick personal fouls on defense, putting Connecticut at the line for the remaining three minutes and twenty-nine seconds and putting Julie in a very precarious position with four fouls. "Stevens better cool off or she's going to be watching the rest of the game from the locker room," says Hall. "Head official Deb Henderson just warned Stevens to stop jawing at the officials. And in my mind, Henderson is one of the best refs in the business. She and the crew today are trying to keep the game in check and let them play, but this is a tough one, folks. It's playoff time in the WNBA! We are going to have an exciting finish," continues Hall.

Kat is now pacing around the room, alternating between watching the game and biting her nails. She's surprised New York Head Coach Moira Clery doesn't pull Julie out for offense instead of defense to protect her four fouls, but then again, Clery is one to let the chips fall where they may. Connecticut calls a timeout with just under two minutes remaining and the game tied at 63. When play resumes, Kat can see Connecticut is going right at Julie with a set play. They isolate Amber Holt on the right wing. Julie's teammate tries to switch with her but Julie shoves her away. Kat can almost read Julie's mind. This is personal now for Julie—it's playground ball and she is not going to switch this matchup this late in the game. Amber pump fakes and drives left, surprising Julie for a split second; she's obviously expecting a drive to the right with Holt's strong hand. Holt gets a step on Julie, pulling up in the lane for a short jumper. Julie tags her on the elbow. Somehow, Holt finishes the play, making the shot as the whistle is blown. Oh no. Oh no. Julie. What have you just done?

"Well, that's it for Julie Stevens. Moira Clery gambled keeping her in for both offense and defense and the gamble just did not pay off. The Liberty are now without their leading scorer for the remaining fifty-nine seconds, and if Amber Holt hits this free throw, they'll also be operating at a three-point deficit," announces Color Analyst Dorothy Hall.

Kat watches Julie take her time walking off the court, giving her team time to convene on the sideline for a moment. Her face is flushed red. She walks down to the end of the bench and puts a towel over her head.

Hall continues, "Finishing the game with twenty-four points, seven rebounds, and five assists, Julie Stevens played well until that hit to the face. She is a bright star in the WNBA, but this is not the first time she's lost her cool during a game, and it may not be the first time it costs her team the game either. This is definitely a part of her personal development as a player that she needs to focus on in the off-season. Her team has to step up for her now or their season will be over."

Kat watches the last minute of play over the next five minutes, with both teams exhausting their timeouts. Down by one, New York has thirteen seconds for one final possession to win the game. Clery calls the play but after a near pick by Connecticut, the play is blown. New York tries to regroup and they get a great shot off the broken play on the left baseline with time expiring. The ball bounces off the rim three excruciating times before rolling out. Connecticut players run to center court in celebration. Before the game cuts to commercial break, Kat sees Julie walking back toward the locker room, alone, the towel still draped over her head.

Kat doesn't even bother waiting for the postgame interviews. She turns off the television and sits quietly with her stomach in knots, wishing she could be there to hold Julie as she exits the locker room, but knowing that ship has sailed.

Chapter Twenty-eight

Julie drives with her old Jeep Wrangler packed up with everything she owns, which isn't much really. One of the not-so-pleasant aspects of being a professional women's basketball player is that you really never have a home for more than a few months at a time. Since the WNBA season is over, Julie is heading back to her parents' house in Utah for some much-needed rest and relaxation.

To her agent's dismay, she makes the decision not to play in the Milano Euroleague for the second season in a row this winter. She needs a break from the game. She needs time to get her mind straight and heal her aching body. She wants to work on her game so that she can come back in 2011 healthy, stronger, and more prepared to take her team all the way.

It took her nearly a week of licking her wounds to even set foot out of her apartment after losing that game three to Connecticut. The worst part was standing by and watching the Connecticut players celebrate at half-court. She took full responsibility in the locker room amongst her teammates and coaches, but they wouldn't hear of it. "We are a team. None of us played or coached a perfect game. None of us did what we needed to do to win the game, Julie. You alone are not at fault," Liberty Head Coach Moira Clery said to her and to the entire team in the locker room after the game. But the coach's words didn't make her feel any better or make the loss hurt any less.

As Julie starts the twenty-three-plus-hour journey on I-80 west from her rented apartment near the New York Liberty training facility in Tarrytown, she doesn't even bother turning on the radio. Her mind is devoid of any basketball thoughts. Instead, there is only one singular, solitary thought bouncing around her brain: 552 Commercial Street Provincetown.

She wonders if deep down that conversation with Molly just a day before the game screwed with her mental mindset so much that it cost her the game and a trip to the Eastern Conference Finals for the first time. Part of her doesn't want to admit the mere idea that Kat loves her could still wreak so much havoc in her life. Part of her also doesn't want to admit that she is so mentally weak she can't put her personal life aside and perform at the highest level when she needs to. Either way you slice it, her mind is a wreck and her heart still hurts so much it's nearly a physical pain in her chest.

The most frustrating thing, the thing she just can't come to terms with, is the fact that Kat apparently loves her but made the choice despite that love to walk away from her career and move to the middle of nowhere in order to avoid Julie.

Julie pulls off to the shoulder of the highway just west of Newark, resting her head on the steering wheel. She is just so tired. Suddenly, she decides on a truly impulsive course of action. She needs closure. She needs to hear Kat explain to her face-to-face why they couldn't be enough so she can move on with her life and try to repair her broken heart.

Carefully pulling back out into traffic, she exits at her first opportunity, sets a new course on her navigation system, and gets moving. By the looks of it, she will reach her new destination in under six hours.

ॐॐॐॐ

Just over four hours later, Julie stops to fill her gas tank and get something to eat. The guy at the gas station recommends a place just across from the Cape Cod Canal called the Seafood Shanty. As she pulls into the parking lot, she sees that guy is onto something. It's in between lunch and dinner but the place it still packed with cars, even though it's late September and most of the summer crowds are gone. It's a no-frills, take-out only place; you either eat in your car or at one of their picnic tables or carry it across the busy street to sit on the banks of the canal.

Before Julie makes her way up to the order window, she decides to roll up the sides and back of her Jeep. It's a gorgeous late September day with the sun still warm in the sky and puffy blue clouds dotting the horizon.

While waiting in line, she asks the guy in front of her what this place is known for. "Clams," he says, smiling. "They make the absolute best fried clams I've ever had. But you can't go wrong with their lobster rolls or fish sandwiches."

"So basically anything on the menu?" Julie asks.

"Yup. Basically," he says, chuckling.

Ten minutes later Julie sits at a nearby picnic table with her whole belly fried clams and a Snapple. The guy in line wasn't kidding. These are bar none the best clams she's ever eaten in her life. As she savors every bite, she soaks in the view of the boats passing by on the canal. She feels warm, peaceful, and oddly calm despite her sudden change in plans and looming interaction with

Kat. She decides to enjoy the afternoon, and if nothing else, knows that her dream of relaxing on a beach is well within reach.

After a phone call home to her parents to let them know of her altered plans, she is back on the road, under two hours from her destination.

Chapter Twenty-nine

Kat cracks one eye open and cringes at the pounding headache that greets her this morning. Her mouth feels like it's cemented shut. Last night she attended her first postseason "townie party." One of the local restaurants puts out a buffet of free food for all the locals so they can relax and enjoy getting their town back after the rigors of tourist season. Abby insisted that Kat attend as a new "townie," but neglected to tell her that first-year townies have to drink whatever shots are purchased for them. After six shots of tequila—which Kat now refers to as Devil Juice—she could barely see straight and had to beg for mercy, citing the fact that there is only a twenty-four-hour clinic in town and not a bona fide hospital.

To her sheer embarrassment, she vaguely recalls dancing with the guys from the Ace Hardware store and the ladies from Mooncusser Tattoos. She shuffles over to the bathroom, downing three Advil and a large glass of water. Cooper looks at her expectantly, but all Kat can manage is to unceremoniously shoo the dog out back, leaving her to her own devices as she pours dry food into her bowl. She holds her head in her hands and groans in distress while she waits for Cooper to do her business. "I will never drink alcohol again," promises Kat to the empty house. Her only consolation is that she has a Saturday filled with absolutely nothing because she has the day off.

Just as she lets Cooper into the house, the phone rings. Kat winces in pain at the mere sound of the ringer.

"Hey, woman. You alive?" Abby asks far too cheerfully.

"Barely," mumbles Kat. "You all nearly killed me last night."

"Ahh, please, a little fun doesn't kill anybody. Listen, I need you to buck up and do me a favor."

"Please tell me this favor has absolutely nothing to do with tequila," Kat says, whimpering.

"Ha. No. Joyce just called. She's sick. Can you fill in for her? I normally would just do it myself, but I have to ride into Truro today.

"Sure, okay, no problem. I just need to get myself together," Kat says, disappointed to lose her sacred day off.

"Take your time. I'll tell Alex at the Wired Puppy to have his famous hangover remedy ready for you."

"Alex has a famous hangover remedy? What is it?"

"He won't say, but he swears it works."

"At this point, I'll try anything." Kat winces as she rubs her head.

"Thanks a million, Kat. Drink water."

"Sure thing."

August felt like a full-out sprint, and with the exception of her two days off with Molly, she worked straight through. That's why she was so looking forward to her day filled with nothing. So much for that.

The warm days of September and October are seen as bonus days for the store owners in Provincetown, with the exception of Women's Week in mid-October. After summer vacation season ends, the town returns to a slower pace, but warm weekends mean tourists in for the weekend or a day, and that translates to additional sales and more money.

Last week Abby took Kat out for a beer at The Squealing Pig to tell her how pleased she was with the summer sales figures. "Sales are up forty-one percent as compared to last year at this time and I attribute that success in large part to you, Kat," said Abby, raising her beer in a toast. "Thank you for everything, Kat. I know you only signed on for the summer, but I'll be open through November and a little bit over the holidays. I want you to know that you have a job with me for as long as you want one. Hell, I'll even give you a raise, and I haven't forgotten about the fee for your photo. How does a fifteen-hundred-dollar bonus sound to you?"

"Wow. Thank you, Abby. I appreciate your taking a chance on me. I have no plans to go anywhere just now, so you're stuck with me for the time being," Kat said with a smirk.

The truth is, Kat has no idea whether she will stay on or go back to her old life as an official. She has put off making any decisions for as long as possible, but time is running out. The WNBA will only honor a leave of absence for a year, and that year is just about up. If she decides to return, she'll have some serious retraining to do, not only to get back in physical shape but also to make sure her officiating legs return to peak form.

Kat is so worn out, she leans up against the back of the shower, letting the hot water pour over her head and down her body. The fact is she could probably sleep standing if it weren't for the memories of a past shower with Julie to wake her up completely.

After she's dressed and as put together as she's going to get, she decides she can't bring herself to walk into town today, so she drives. She stops at the Wired Puppy and picks up the mysteriously famous hangover remedy from Alex. He laughs when he sees the dark circles under her eyes as she gingerly lifts her sunglasses. "Ahh, you've got that first-year townie party afterglow," he says. "This is the tenth one I've made so far this morning."

"Thanks," Kat whispers, putting down a five-dollar bill on the counter.

"No, no, this one's on the house. It's the least I can do after the torture they put you through, especially the dancing with Mike and Dave."

Kat is thoroughly embarrassed to be remembered for her dancing with the Ace Hardware guys. "Oh, I was hoping that didn't really happen," she says weakly.

"Oh, it happened. Don't look on Facebook. There are more than a few pictures of you guys dancing cheek to cheek to Madonna," Alex says, snorting.

"Wonderful." Kat walks out the door, mentally thinking to check Facebook later.

Just as she gets to her car, she hears someone whistle. She looks up and sees Dave across the street yelling some Madonna lyrics. In his best falsetto, he implores a DJ to play some dance tunes and waves as he walks down the street laughing. Some other guy a few feet away picks up the tune and continues singing it.

"I'm never going to live this down," Kat says to Cooper as they climb back in the car.

Because she has so much on her mind, Kat is relieved that Abby's gallery is a little quieter today. And she will be forever indebted to Alex and his magical hangover remedy. Whatever is in that thing is magical juice that needs to be bottled and sold.

The stream of shoppers is slow but steady so she definitely has time to make sure the books are in order. She even takes time to clean the desk area, reorganizing the drawers and files. She glances over to Cooper who is sound asleep on her bed behind the desk, totally comfortable.

Kat thinks about what would happen to Cooper if she returned to officiating. Cooper is her constant companion and she winces at the thought of having to board her or send her off to Molly's every time she has a road trip. Cooper alone might be her deciding factor, as crazy at it sounds. The voice of reason in her mind says *Don't make career decisions based on the dog*, but then the other voice in her mind—the one she's been listening to more of late—whispers, *Why not make career decisions, including the well-being of my loved ones, such as Cooper?*

Kat takes a second to scan the empty gallery. Could this be enough for her? Could she really be content living her year-round, running someone else's gallery? Her needs are minimal here. It's not like she needs to pull in six figures. She's learned to live simply and with meaning. Part of her misses the pace and excitement of her work as an official, but part of her believes the person she used to be is gone. She's reinvented herself here in Provincetown and feels more comfortable in her own skin than she has in a long time.

The phone rings, knocking Kat out of her reverie.

"Carmichael Gallery, how can I help you?"

"Hey, babe. How's it going?"

"Hey, Abby," Kat replies, a little surprised to receive a check-in call from Abby. "Is something wrong?"

"No, no of course not. Listen, I feel bad about asking you to come in today after all the fun you had last night. How busy is it?"

"It's been slow. I sold a couple of small prints."

"Okay. Close up. Take what's left of the afternoon

off. I know it's not much, but at least the day won't be a total loss for you."

"Are you sure? I really don't mind staying; I'm actually feeling much better. That hangover remedy did the trick."

"I'm sure. Pack it in. Joyce says she's feeling better and can cover tomorrow, so I'll see you Monday."

"Okay great, Abby. Thanks so much!"

Kat wastes no time closing up the store. In ten minutes flat, the lights are off and the place is locked down. Once outside, she looks up at the clear blue sky. It's a perfect day in P-Town. She feels the light breeze and the still-warm sun and immediately decides to take a walk through town and maybe even stop for a drink at the Aqua Bar with Cooper. Cooper looks up at her, a little surprised to be taking a left on Commercial Street instead of their typical right to head home.

"C'mon, Cooper, let's do some shopping and enjoy the day," Kat says, her tone light.

Cooper wags her tail in assent and the two head off up the street.

Chapter Thirty

Julie passes Kat's house three times, slowing each time in front of the mailbox before feeling like a stalker and zooming off. After her third drive by, she changes course and squeezes into a parking spot on Commercial Street only a few houses past Kat's. Too afraid to actually walk up the steps to the house, she decides to take things slow by going for a walk in the other direction instead.

This is Julie's first time in Provincetown, although several of her friends have been trying to get her here for years, especially for Women's Week that is held every year in mid-October. Despite the fact that she travels all over the world for basketball, this place immediately feels comfortable to her. She walks down the narrow Commercial Street, looking at the clapboard houses and the intricate shapes of stars and half-moons cut out on the shutters. Every house has character, and some have pretty, well-maintained gardens. She observes a few random things like garden gnomes wearing rainbow T-shirts or a pair of boots oddly hanging from an upstairs window, but even the strange seems to fit in perfectly here.

As she gets closer to the center of town, she notices a few interesting art galleries. She's prompted to enter and walk around a few of them, even though she's not normally drawn to modern art. She picks her way slowly through town, stopping here and there to check out a shop or stop to look at the stunning view of the water half-hidden down small sand-lined alleyways in between houses. She gets a cup of coffee at a place called the Wired Puppy and is amazed to see a guy with a long black beard stroll in with a Siamese cat perched across his shoulders. Apparently, the guy and the cat are regulars because no one seems to pay them any mind as the man orders a cup of tea and waits reading the local paper. Julie laughs at the cat because it looks so comfortable and at ease lying across the guy's shoulders like a shawl.

She continues up Commercial Street, sipping her coffee, stopping for a minute to listen to an older woman playing classical guitar music on the street. Julie breathes in the salt air and looks up at the clear blue sky. Even though her nerves are a mess at the thought of seeing Kat, Provincetown starts doing to her what it does to everyone who walks down its streets—it lures her in; it forces her to relax, take a deep breath, and enjoy the moment. She realizes why Kat came here but pushes the thought from her mind; the mere thought of Kat's name tangles her stomach in knots.

She walks down MacMillan Wharf, taking in the sights and sounds when a large framed print hanging in the window of a photography gallery on the corner catches her eye. There is a woman in the photo, with long black hair flying in the wind as she stares at the ocean at sunset. Julie crosses the street to get a closer look. From across the street, she swears the woman in the photograph looks just like Kat. As she gets closer to examine the photo, she literally stops in her tracks. It is Kat. Julie has the sensation of her heart slamming into her chest. She cannot take her eyes off this photograph. She is so stunned to see Kat's profile hanging in the gallery, she is unable to move, to think. All she can do is look at Kat's face. A small dog barks as it passes with its owner jolting Julie out of her bodily freeze. She looks up at the sign: Carmichael Gallery. She walks to the door and pulls the handle only to realize it's locked. The hanging in the window reads, "Closed Now. Back Tomorrow."

Julie sits down on the step in front of the gallery trying to collect her thoughts. Whatever spell Provincetown put on her as she strolled through town has been unceremoniously lifted. The photograph of Kat is a glaring representation that she has made a new life for herself here in Provincetown. A new life that Julie doesn't fit into. Julie drove here partly thinking, partly hoping, that maybe Kat was unhappy in Provincetown. Maybe she was lonely. Perhaps she felt as out of sorts as Julie did. But after looking long and hard at that photograph, Julie feels like a fool. Kat isn't pining for her. Kat is here living her life the way she wants it: without Julie. Now, she knows. Now, she can see for herself that whatever Julie thought they had meant absolutely nothing to Kat. She is an absolute idiot for coming here.

She wants nothing more than to climb into her Jeep and speed as far away from Provincetown as she can, but she realizes her car is parked way back down Commercial Street, meaning she has to walk the entire way back to her car before she can get out of here and finally try to put this place and Kat out of her mind for good. With her head down and her hands in her pockets, she begins the long walk back to her car.

꙳꙳꙳꙳

Kat and Cooper walk home after a leisurely afternoon in town. Kat bought a few unusual items at her favorite store, Roots, and Cooper even scored with a nondairy peanut butter doggie ice cream. Kat is relaxed and thoroughly enjoying this lazy, warm afternoon. Town is the perfect blend of bustling but not crazy, a welcome departure from the hectic summer.

As they pass the gallery once more on their way back down Commercial Street, Kat is tempted to go back in and reopen for the evening. She stops for a moment and looks down at Cooper looking up at her expectantly. "Nope," she says aloud to Cooper. "We are not going back to work. We are going home to enjoy the evening."

Once they walk through the center of town, heading toward the East End, the shops dwindle and are replaced by clapboard homes with neat gardens, a few inns, and art galleries. Fewer people walk this far down Commercial Street, and this time of year and day, fewer cars pass by, so it feels like they have the entire street to themselves. Kat takes in the houses and their gardens, the rainbow flags and the bikes leaning against fence posts. She soaks in the September day and is aware of how relaxed and comfortable she is to be alone. It's a clear and sweet feeling, and she knows this place is simply good for her soul.

Kat notices Cooper's pace quicken. She looks up to see a person about twenty yards ahead of them. She smiles at Cooper. That dog is such a ham. She sees an opportunity for a new person to pet her and picks up the pace to catch up. Since Kat is in such a generous mood, she picks up her pace too, letting Cooper lead her on.

As they get within ten feet of the woman ahead of them, Kat spots the short white blond hair. She notices the woman's height, the athletic build. This little voice in her head whispers *Julie.* Kat is struck so off guard by it, she doesn't see the cracked edge of the sidewalk and she trips. Hard. She literally flies face first, catching her fall with her knees and her wrists, slamming onto the ground. Cooper begins to bark excitedly partly thinking Kat is playing a new game. She lifts her head. The woman ahead of her turns around, hearing the commotion. Kat's not sure if she hit her head or not, but she can swear the woman looking at her is Julie.

Julie has a look on her face of sheer and utter terror. Kat lies in the street, her eyes fixed on her. Julie freezes for a moment, seemingly unsure whether to run away or run toward Kat.

Kat cries out, "Julie? Is that you?" She struggles to stand. Her two palms are scraped raw and bloody. Both of her knees are bleeding badly. Julie just stands there, her face ashen as she stares back at her.

Julie turns away and starts walking, her movements jerky. She dashes to her Jeep and appears to struggle with unlocking it.

Kat ignores the ringing in her ears and limps after her.

"Julie! Please! Stop!" Kat yells as she catches up with Julie and leans against Julie's Jeep. "It is you. Right? I'm not making this up in my head. Julie?"

"Yeah, it's me." Julie practically spits the words. She stops again, turning back to look at Kat and Kat stares back at her. Kat is immediately lost in those endless blue-green eyes and finally understands why she loves the beaches in Provincetown so much—on just the right day with just the right amount of sun, the water looks exactly the same color as Julie's eyes. Kat wobbles forward, and Julie reaches out to catch her.

"Whoa. You're not too steady. Did you hit your

head?"

"I'm not sure, to be honest. My house is right there." Kat points just up ahead.

"I know," Julie replies, still holding Kat up.

"How do you know?" Kat asks, feeling as though she's going to pass out any minute. *I don't think this is real. This can't be real*, thinks Kat.

"You're bleeding pretty bad. Let me help you get into the house, okay?"

"Okay," whispers Kat. "That's Cooper."

"Cooper? As in Cynthia Cooper?"

"You're the only one who's ever guessed that on the first try." Kat grins, still staring at Julie.

"Go figure," Julie says wryly as they slowly climb the stairs to Kat's house, with Kat leaning heavily on Julie.

Once inside, Kat sits down while Julie grabs some wet paper towels from the kitchen. "Here. Use these. Do you have a first-aid kit?"

"Yeah, in the bathroom. First door on the left." Kat begins to wipe the blood from her legs.

Julie returns a moment later with a massive first-aid kit. "Do you work as an EMT part-time? This thing is huge."

Kat laughs, but it hurts her head. "No, it was on sale at the hardware store. I couldn't resist. You never know."

"Apparently."

Julie kneels down in front of Kat, rummaging through the kit. She finds alcohol wipes and tears a couple open. "This is going to hurt a little." The instant the wipes make contact with Kat's knees, she winces in pain.

Neither speaks as Julie gently cleans out the

wounds on Kat's legs, applying ointment and large Band-Aids. She turns her attention to Kat's palms, which are in worse shape. Bits of dirt and debris are stuck in the cuts. Kat can't feel a thing as Julie holds her hand to clean it up, even though she knows she should. All she can do is stare at Julie's face, her cheeks, her nose, and her beautiful lips. She can't believe that after all this time, Julie is here in her house touching her. Kat breathes in the smell of Julie's shampoo and it sends tingles down her spine.

Once Julie seems convinced the first palm is clean, she repeats the steps of applying ointment and Band-Aid before beginning the same process with the other palm. With one hand free, Kat can't help but reach out to touch Julie. She runs her fingers through her hair and down her jawbone. Kat is so lost in the moment, she is flat out surprised when Julie jerks her head away.

"Please, Kat. Let me finish this," Julie says tersely.

After a few more minutes of awkward silence, Julie finishes Kat's other hand. She cleans everything up, puts the first-aid kit away, and washes her hands. She pours a glass of water and returns to Kat with the water in hand and two Advil.

"You should take these and you should probably ice your knees. I'm sure they are going to swell up."

Kat takes the Advil and downs the glass of water, suddenly realizing how thirsty she is. She leans back on the couch and rubs her head where she must've hit it.

"Are you still dizzy?"

"No. Not dizzy. Just really, really embarrassed and totally shocked to see you," Kat says.

"You might have a mild concussion. Just don't go taking any naps for the rest of the day," Julie responds, neglecting to address any of Kat's other points.

"Well, there goes my plan for the rest of the afternoon," Kat says with a sigh.

"Okay then. I guess I'll be going." Julie starts walking for the door.

"Wait. You're leaving? Just like that?" Kat stands quickly and feels her head pound. "You can't just leave, Julie. Please, sit down."

Julie stands at the door and Kat can see a world of emotion passing through her eyes, but Julie says nothing. After a few moments, she sits stiffly across from Kat.

"So…" says Kat.

"So…" says Julie.

"Why are you here? I mean I'm glad you're here, but I just wasn't expecting it, obviously."

Julie sighs and looks down at her hands. "To see you." She pauses. "I drove by your place a few times and chickened out. I decided to walk through town instead."

"Oh," is all Kat manages. Maybe she hit her head harder than she thought, but she doesn't remember ever giving Julie her new address here in P-Town. "But how did you know where to find me?"

"Right. Your great disappearing act. You didn't think anyone would ever find you here, I'm sure," says Julie sarcastically.

"No, that's not what I meant. I'm glad you're here," she says slowly to make sure Julie doesn't mistake her meaning. "Julie, it's good to see you."

Julie stands as if poised to take flight, her eyes blinking rapidly. "It's good to see me? Really? Is it? You don't see me for almost a year and when you do, you take a giant header in the road."

"Well, I was. I mean I am more than a little surprised. You knocked me off my feet," Kat says, trying humor. Julie doesn't bite.

"I'm sure you are. It's not every day the woman you ran away from shows up to pick you up off the pavement," Julie says coldly.

"Ouch," is all Kat can say.

"Yeah. Ouch is right." Julie crosses her arms across her chest and stares at Kat before continuing. "Do you ever even think of me? I mean here you are in this perfect little beach town with a brand new life and a dog for Christ's sakes."

Kat looks at Julie, her heartbeat racing. Her knees are throbbing and her hand is killing her. All of the pent-up anger she saw in Julie whenever she watched her play basketball on television is ready to burst forth, and Kat knows it. She knows whatever she says next will determine if she can fix what she broke.

"Well? Do you?" Julie demands.

Kat rises and walks to her. She gently pulls Julie's crossed arms down and gingerly holds her hands. Julie begins to pull away but Kat doesn't budge. "I love you." That's what she chooses to say. No big explanation.

"What?" Julie's voice is shaking.

"I hurt you badly, and I am so sorry. Julie, I love you. From a place so deep I can't reach in and stop it. I really made a mess of things, but I love you with all my heart and with all my soul," Kat says quietly as she looks deep into Julie's eyes.

Tears stream down Julie's face. Kat leans forward to kiss them away. She wants so much to remove all the pain she's caused her. As she tastes Julie's tears, she wants so much for Julie to see her as she is now—open and willing and able to finally commit to a life together.

Julie roughly pulls herself away from Kat.

"Are you fucking kidding me? No, really. Is this

some stupid joke?" Julie's face reddens, as she shakes with rage. "Let me get this straight. We meet. We connect. We fall in love or, at least, I fall in love. I tell you how I feel. You bolt. And you don't just go under the radar for a while, but you actually quit your job—the kind of job people kill for—so you don't need to see me." Julie paces around the small room and continues her rant. "You move away and don't tell anyone where you are going. Well, you tell Molly. You never figured she would tell me where you were, did you?"

Kat can't hide the surprise at the mention of Molly's name. "Well she did," says Julie. "That little fucker decides to tell me where you are the day before game three against Connecticut."

Now Kat begins to put the pieces together, and the knowledge dawns on her. She knew something was wrong with Julie during that game.

"I wrote you letters. I texted you. Nothing. You didn't respond to anything."

"Wait, Julie. I never got any letters. My mail never forwarded correctly. I had to turn in my work cell phone so I got a new phone and a new number," Kat says, pleading.

Julie rages on as if she doesn't hear Kat's explanation. "You start a whole new fucking life here at the beach, apparently modeling or some shit, and only after I pick you up literally as you nearly break your ass you tell me you love me? You're sorry? Really? This must be a fucking joke."

"I'm sorry, modeling?" Kat asks, trying to keep up with the barrage of words flying out of Julie's mouth at warp speed.

"I saw that photo of you in town. You're on the beach. It's sunset. At first, I didn't realize it was you;

then I got up close and knew. I tried to go into the gallery but it was closed."

"Julie, I'm not a model. I work at that gallery. Abby is the photographer and she took that photo earlier in the summer."

"Oh, so your new girlfriend just couldn't wait to take some photos of her hot new piece of ass." Julie sneers.

Kat openly laughs at that remark. "Julie, if you saw Abby, you would realize how ridiculous that comment is. I don't have any girlfriend. Abby is a friend and my boss. That's it."

"Whatever."

"Can I explain? Will you let me explain all of this to you? Because I want to."

"I don't want to hear your explanations. I don't want to hear any of it." Julie races to the door and sprints out of Kat's house before Kat can stop her. Kat runs to her window and sees Julie jump into her Jeep. The tires squeal as she pulls away.

Kat stands in the window, staring at the place where Julie's car was parked. Her head is swimming, her knees and hands are killing her, but it's nothing compared to the headache and the heartache she feels. If she had only been prepared to see Julie. If she only knew she was coming, she could have been ready. She would have known what to say.

Kat picks up her cell phone and texts Molly. "You told Julie where I live?"

She waits for a response. Nothing. She throws the phone on the couch. A few moments later she hears the phone beep.

"I did."

"She was here," types Kat.

"Was?"

"Long story. Told her I loved her. She ran."

"Go find her!" Molly texts back.

"No clue where she went."

"Go find her," repeats Molly.

"Btw I'm mad at you," types Kat.

"I know. But it had to be done."

"You could have warned me first," responds Kat.

"Why ruin the surprise?"

Kat throws the phone back on the couch. She has absolutely no idea where Julie went. For all she knows, Julie is long gone on Route 6 on her way back to New York. She knows calling her or texting her is useless. She needs to clean herself up and take stock of the situation. She needs a plan.

Chapter Thirty-one

Julie drives aimlessly through town until she sees the signs for the National Seashore. She knows she is too emotionally wrung out to drive anywhere for long so she decides her best course of action is to take some time to get herself back together first. She steers past the sand dunes slowly until she sees signs for Race Point. She's never been there before, but it sounds promising enough.

After parking her car, she walks down a huge sand dune path to the ocean and is immediately struck by the sheer vastness of the beach. A few people are walking back, but Julie drops her head, unwilling to make eye contact with anyone right now.

She walks for a while on the beach until she is just too tired to keep going. She sits down and stares into the water. What the hell just happened? Never could she have imagined the possibility that Kat would say she is sorry and loves her. She had just assumed that Kat left her because Kat didn't want to be with her. But Kat's admission is so unexpected it sends Julie reeling. She's not proud of the way she blew up at her. In fact, she's embarrassed by it. But it's the truth. She is angry with Kat. She has been nursing a broken heart for so many months it's become a hobby for her and fodder for her play on the court.

At just twenty-three years old, Julie has never experienced intense emotions like this for anyone. She's been with women before, although never for more than a few months at a time, and knew she was gay from birth, basically, but love—well that's a different story. Kat is truly her first love and her first real heartbreak. Because these are all uncharted waters for her, she just doesn't know how to deal with the swirl of emotions. She wishes she could just walk away and feel nothing, but she knows now it's not possible.

If Kat really loves her so much, why did she wait for Julie to come to her? Julie wonders as she stares into the endless ocean that looks gray, mirroring her mood and nearly matching the exact smoky-gray color of Kat's eyes. The thing is, Julie isn't interested in playing the field or having a bunch of meaningless one-night stands. She grew up in a home filled with love. She saw the way her parents looked at one another and still do. She knew love her entire life and she knows the real deal when she sees it. She was so sure when she met Kat for the first time. She was certain that she and Kat fit together perfectly. Their immediate connection was something that took on a life of its own so quickly, Julie never stopped to question it, or them, until it was too late and Kat had run away.

Well, if you're going to run away, I guess this is the place to run to, Julie admits to herself. She can see why and how Kat would have been drawn to the allure of Provincetown. It's the exact polar opposite of daily life in the WNBA with the raucous arenas, traffic, and impersonal hotel rooms.

But now, she doubts her instincts at all. How could she make a life with someone she's afraid will leave her the moment things get complicated or difficult? How can she ever forgive Kat? Because it's going to take true and utter forgiveness for them to ever have a fighting chance to be together.

≈≈≈≈

Thirty minutes later, Kat is showered—not a pleasant experience with her burning palms and knees. It's getting chilly, so she throws on an old faded pair of jeans and her favorite and lucky Notre Dame sweatshirt that definitely shows its age by way of frayed cuffs and torn neckline. She takes the extra five minutes to apply a small amount of makeup. Nothing crazy, because if she does find Julie, she doesn't want to look all made up. She feeds Cooper dinner a little early and leaves her with a marrowbone and a movie playing on the Hallmark Channel. Just in case she'll be gone for a while, she leaves a few lights on.

Kat drives slowly through town, looking for Julie's Jeep along side streets, in public lots, or small inn parking spaces. Julie's red Jeep Wrangler won't be tough to spot if she only knows where to look. She continues all the way up Commercial Street until it ends. She loops onto Route 6 and decides to detour through Herring Cove. With only four cars parked in the huge beach lot, Kat circles quickly and decides to continue on to Race Point Beach. The road that connects the two beaches is cut through the sand dunes, making it feel like you're passing through a moonscape. The sun is setting early, hinting at the oncoming winter, Kat notes as she drives past the small airport up to the Race Point lot.

She is partly surprised and partly not surprised at all to see Julie's red Jeep Wrangler parked in the lot. After she parks, she peeks in the windows to see the car jammed with stuff. No Julie. Kat grabs a blanket from the back of her car before heading out down the huge dune to the beach itself.

The view at Race Point Beach never fails to ignite the senses. The sheer expanse of beach is truly magnificent. For as far as the eye can see in either direction there is nothing but ocean and sand. Kat works her way downhill toward the beach, noting that walking in deep loose sand is not helping her increasingly sore knees. As she reaches the more compact sand closer to the water, she sees Julie sitting alone far down the beach, staring into the water. It takes Kat several minutes, but she finally makes her way over to Julie. While she walks, she thinks of what she can say to fix it all. She doesn't even know how to start.

"Do you mind if I sit down?"

Julie jumps at the sound of Kat's voice but doesn't turn to look at her. "Go ahead," is all she says.

Kat sits in the sand to Julie's left, hugging her knees to her chest. The wind off the water is definitely chilly. Kat looks over to Julie who is still wearing shorts and a T-shirt. She must be freezing, Kat thinks. She resists the urge to drape her blanket over Julie's shoulders.

"I have a blanket if you're cold," Kat says.

"I'm fine," Julie answers stubbornly, although Kat can see from the goose bumps on her arms that she's freezing. "How did you find me?"

"Well, a red Jeep Wrangler with Utah plates that read Hoops 15 isn't exactly tough to spot," Kat says. "Plus, this is where I go when I need to clear my head too."

"All season long, all I could think about was coming to a place like this to relax and stop thinking. Now I'm here and I can't relax or stop thinking," muses Julie.

Kat starts to say something but decides against it.

Instead, she elects to let Julie dictate the conversation. She's in no rush and she knows if she pushes too hard Julie will run again. The two sit silently, listening to the crashing waves as the tide recedes for a few minutes before Julie speaks again.

"I just don't understand how you could walk away so easily," Julie says finally, her voice shaky as she continues to stare out at the water.

"It wasn't easy," Kat says matter-of-factly. "It was the hardest thing I've ever done, but something was broken with me and I needed to fix it."

"You know what I keep replaying over and over in my mind?"

"What?"

"When we made love against your front door. Over and over again I see us there and feel you come. I hear me say I love you. And I see your eyes well up but then I don't know what I missed. What did I miss, Kat? How did I get everything so wrong?"

"You got all of it right," Kat says honestly. "Julie that was the problem. I'm not sure how I can explain this to you."

"Try. Please, for my sake. Because I feel like I can't trust myself anymore. I can't trust my heart or my instincts because all I keep thinking is how did I make such a huge mistake."

Kat notices that Julie is visibly shivering now. She thinks about how similar she once felt when Danielle left her and how she felt she couldn't trust her instincts then either. Before she continues, she opens the blanket and wraps it around Julies shoulders, tucking it in around her legs and sides. If Julie is appreciative of the gesture, she doesn't show it.

Kat watches a few waves roll in while she thinks

of how to explain everything to Julie. "Things with us happened really fast. You didn't miss anything or misread any situation. What I feel for you is incredibly powerful and real. I think I fell in love with you after that first kiss in the bar, to be honest with you, and I'm in love with you after all this time apart. It scared me, Julie, for a few reasons. Danielle left me just when I thought things were fine between us. And, while deep down I know now that she was right to do it, it brought up a lot of stuff that I never really dealt with." Kat shifts in the sand, trying to get all of the jumbled nonsense in her head to make sense aloud.

She continues, "You started asking questions about my family but I never really answered you. I never knew my dad. He left when I was just six years old, but from what I gather, he was a loser. I don't even remember him except for his mustache and his deep voice, of all things. My mom was a raging drug addict and alcoholic. Even though I lived with her like that for years, working jobs to pay our bills, she wasn't a mom to me. Then she died and I moved in with Molly and her family. The feelings I had for you brought up all of this. I was terrified you would see that I was a mess of a person and you would leave me too."

"But—" Julie interrupts her.

"No, wait, let me finish," says Kat. "Then we were sitting in that diner and you were talking to me about playing overseas in Italy, and I was so proud and happy for you. But as a former player who always wanted to play pro and never got the chance, I was also a little jealous. And I knew if things were reversed, I would move heaven and earth to be in the position you are as a player. I refused to be the reason for you not fulfilling your dreams as a basketball player. I thought that if I walked away before things got too serious you would be able to continue playing wherever you wanted and not be bogged down with a relationship."

Kat takes a deep breath and decides she might as well let it all hang out. "Finally, I was terrified about what the league would do if they found out we were together. I would have been fired and you might have been suspended. I thought the best course of action was to take a leave of absence so I could figure out what to do next. Plus, I had to get out of my house. It was suffocating me. Danielle and I bought it together and I just felt so weighed down by my past, I knew I had to figure myself out before I would be of any use to you."

Julie is silent for a while, so long in fact that Kat begins to think she made a mistake by telling her all of it.

After a few minutes, Julie says, "And you didn't think to tell me any of this? You just made the decision for us without even discussing it with me."

"You're right. I did. I was wrong. I've always had to figure things out on my own, and I know I tend to be a little stubborn."

"A little?"

"I never really dealt with any of this, Julie. I never dealt with my mom's dying because I was so focused on getting a scholarship and playing basketball. I never really dealt with Danielle leaving me. I just threw myself into work. I never really dealt with anything. I know you think coming out here was crazy. Believe me, you're not the only one. But this place has been good for me. Really good, actually."

"Working at an art gallery is good for you?" Julie asks.

"Yeah. It is. My degree from Notre Dame is in business. I run the gallery and I like it a lot more than

I thought I would. I'm good at it too. I get to meet new people, and best of all, I don't have to travel farther than down the street. And, I get to spend time with Cooper."

"Do you miss it?"

"Of course I miss it. I dream of playing and of making calls. I watched every one of your games like five times each."

Julie turns to look at Kat when she says this. "You did?"

"Yes, of course I did. I saw the game against Connecticut. Everyone was talking about your performance as record breaking, but all I could see was the broken heart I caused and it made me sick."

"Yeah. All of it was for you. Stupid, I know." Julie tosses little rocks into the water.

"Not stupid," Kat says softly. "I knew it was. I felt all of it. Julie, I'm so sorry."

"Please, stop apologizing. I don't want your pity."

"I'm not pitying you. I mean it. I know I screwed up. I can't promise that I won't screw up again, but I do promise to be better and to talk to you before I make any crazy stupid decisions."

"That's providing we talk beyond this conversation. You're taking a lot for granted," Julie replies.

The unexpected comment stings Kat, pulling her back into herself.

"I'm sorry, that was uncalled for," Julie says, softening. "Look. I came here under some crazy delusion that I needed closure. I needed to hear you say it was over, but you're not saying that and I just don't know how to react to all of this. It's a lot to take in." She pauses and takes a deep breath before asking her final question.

"Why didn't you come to me if this is how you

really feel? What if Molly never gave me your address? Would you ever come find me?"

"I honestly don't know the answer to that," Kat says. "So many times I thought about reaching out to you, but I saw the anger in your eyes when I watched you play on television and I knew that anger was directed at me. I guess I just assumed you hated me and never wanted anything to do with me after what I did."

"I don't hate you, Kat."

"Look, I know I have to earn your trust again if you let me. But in the meantime, it's absolutely freezing and it's pretty dark. Why don't we go back to my place? I promise I'll give you all the space you need. You can have the guest room. It doesn't make sense for you to drive anywhere tonight. Okay?"

"I am frozen solid," Julie admits to her.

Chapter Thirty-two

Kat lies in bed staring up at the ceiling trying her damnedest not to think about Julie lying just a few feet away in the next room. The mere thought of Julie occupying this space changes not only Kat's energy but also the energy inside her home. It's both uncomfortable and perfect, simultaneously. Julie is right: her knees are a little swollen and she should have iced them, but after their conversation on the beach, it seemed the best thing to do was retreat to respective corners. Since her house is so small, the only semblance of respective corners are the two separate bedrooms, aligned side by side.

Kat is buoyed by the fact that she was utterly and completely honest with Julie. She set aside her fears and insecurities and told Julie exactly what caused her to leave. She was clear that she wanted to make things work, and she was absolutely crystal clear that she loved her, loves her still.

Yet, truth aside, the future is what still concerns Kat. On one hand, she knows that if Julie tells her that too much water has passed under the bridge, she will be okay. She may never love like that again, but she will be okay, regardless of whether she returns to officiating or she stays in Provincetown.

On the other hand, what if Julie comes back to her? Then what? As much as she wants this, it scares her to death. She's not sure if a long-distance relationship will even work with Julie's grueling schedule, nor does it make sense to return to officiating if that happens. Part of her doesn't want to be forced into making that decision with officiating because of their relationship. She wants that choice to be hers and hers alone. Kat's mind continues to circle round and round until the sound of the ocean surf lulls her into a deep and dreamless sleep.

❧❧❧❧

Kat isn't sure when it happened, but at some point during the night, Julie must have climbed into bed with her. Kat knows this because she awakens to the sound of birds outside the window and when she opens her eyes, she realizes that she is wrapped completely around Julie in the big spoon position. Her left arm is snuggled over Julie's shoulder and tucked under her right side; her left leg is wrapped over Julie. She takes a moment to breathe in the morning air and that scent that is all Julie. She is afraid to move a muscle because Julie is sleeping deeply, her breath long and low.

This is heaven on earth, thinks Kat, as she watches Julie sleep. She's never noticed the subtle freckles on the bridge of Julie's nose before and each one fascinates her as if they are their own little universes. This has to be a good sign, Kat thinks. This has to be a signal that Julie heard what she said last night and is trying to show Kat her true feelings.

Kat watches the clock turn to seven and as if on cue, Cooper pops her head up and throws a paw on the bed. This is Cooper's normal morning ritual that begins promptly at seven. Kat isn't quite sure how a dog can tell time, but this one clearly can. Again, Cooper flings her paw on the bed, near Julie's face and the motion wakes Julie up. Kat watches her eyes flutter open and focus on Cooper's panting in her face.

"Well hello, Cooper," whispers Julie. "I guess you want breakfast?" Julie turns to look at Kat to see if she is awake. When she sees Kat looking at her, she smiles shyly, simply saying, "Hi."

"Hi," Kat says, her eyes softening.

"So, I'm guessing it's Cooper time?"

"Something like that." Kat laughs. "And if I ignore her, she just becomes more relentless. Give me fifteen minutes. Please don't move. I'll be back. I promise." She resists the urge to kiss Julie, but decides to wait just in case Julie is still having second thoughts.

Kat hops out of bed, feeling the soreness in her knees and hands from yesterday's spill, and pats Cooper on the head. "Okay, okay, I'm up. Let's go outside."

She throws on a pair of sweats and takes Cooper outside for an abbreviated walk on the beach. It's a foggy morning, with the Long Point lighthouse horn blowing every fifteen seconds. The sound is comforting to Kat in an odd sort of way. It's as if even in the thickest fog, that lighthouse will protect her from getting lost—both literally and figuratively. About halfway from their normal turnaround point, she stops and whistles for Cooper who is busy chasing a few wood ducks further down the beach. Cooper runs to her immediately, a little perplexed to be turning back so soon.

True to her word, almost fifteen minutes later to the second, Kat returns to the bedroom to see Julie sound asleep, and her heart fills up all over again. She wonders if that feeling would ever get old or dissipate if they were together for many years, and she doubts it would ever be so. She starts to walk back out of the room to give Julie time to sleep in but then decides against it. I told her I was coming back and so I will, she thinks, slipping under the covers next to her.

Moments later, Julie slowly turns over so they are facing one another, each lying on their sides, nearly touching but not. Julie opens her eyes and looks at Kat with an expression so filled with love that Kat nearly begins to cry. Kat matches her and tries to show her without touching or speaking how much she loves her too. Then she gently runs her index finger down the side of Julie's face and leaves her hand resting on Julie's shoulder. Julie brushes a loose strand of hair away from Kat's face. They both take a deep breath as if inhaling the other so that their breathing is synched. Kat feels like it's an eternity before Julie leans forward to kiss her. The kiss is so gentle at first Kat isn't even sure their lips are entirely touching. It's a kiss filled with sweetness and innocence and so much love that Kat has to fight back self-inflicting anger at how she could have been so stupid as to hurt such a beautiful soul. Kat returns the kiss, afraid to press for more, but wanting desperately for their bodies to be touching.

Julie pulls away first and Kat can see tears streaming down her face.

"Please, please don't hurt me like that again, Kat. I don't think I'll survive it," Julie whispers, barely loud enough for Kat to hear.

Every ounce of self-control Kat has shown to this point is hurled out the window. She just cannot wait another second before touching Julie, feeling her, kissing her, showing her how deep her love truly runs.

"I love you. I love you so much," Kat whispers as she pulls Julie on top of her, both of her bruised hands on either side of Julie's face. Kat kisses her fully, openly, and without reservation and, now, Julie doesn't pull back but leans into the kiss, matching it. In one motion, Kat gingerly pulls off Julie's T-shirt and begins running her fingers up and down Julie's back. Julie rises up enough to pull off Kat's tank top. Just the feeling of skin on skin sends Kat into another stratosphere. Julie touches her softly, reverently almost. With each touch, Kat tells her how much she loves her, and Julie responds in kind. While they have experienced some serious sexual chemistry in the past, this time, it's very different. This time, their hearts are wide open to each other without fear and with full disclosure. This isn't just sex for the chemical reaction, this is sex with their hearts and souls mixed in.

Kat sits up with Julie straddling her. "I want to look at you," Kat says simply as she kisses Julie's jaw, her neck, her throat. When her lips make contact with Julie's nipples, Julie shudders. Kat takes her nipple in her mouth, rolling her tongue back and forth. Julie's head tips back. Kat moves to her other nipple, teasing, sucking, and kissing until Julie moans.

"Kiss me," Julie urges her. Kat barely lets her finish the command before her lips are there, their breathing hot and ragged, their tongues tangling and untangling. Julie's hands have free rein and roam over Kat's body, front to back. Kat pulls Julie closer, their bodies beginning to rock in unison. Kat's hand works down inside of Julie's underwear; at the same time, Julie pulls at Kat's Calvin Klein boy shorts. Something inside Kat's mind clicks into place when her fingers plunge deep inside of Julie only to feel how incredibly wet she is. Julie's fingers reach deep inside of Kat as the two hold onto each other with their free hands. Kat can feel her muscles open up to receive more and more of

Julie's hand, and Julie's body reacts in similar fashion.

"Look at me," Julie whispers, as they rock together.

Kat opens her eyes and is immediately lost inside those immaculate blue-green eyes. She starts to feel a tingling sensation in her toes and begins to arch forward, tightening. "Stay here with me," Julie urges her again as she thrusts her hips forward into Kat, grinding Kat's fingers and hand deeper into her. The orgasm that rocks Kat over the next thirty seconds is longer, deeper, and more intense than anything she has ever felt, including all previous times with Julie. And the strength of it seems to grow exponentially as she sees Julie climaxing with her at exactly the same instant. Both throw their heads back, crying out in ecstasy, locked into each other, shuddering over and over again until Kat can no longer hold Julie up; she falls back on the bed, with Julie collapsing on top of her. Both still have their fingers inside the other.

They lay like this for several minutes, taking time for their breathing to return to normal. Julie shifts first, removing her fingers. She pulls Kat's hand free and draws both of Kat's hands up over her head. Now, they are pressed body to body, touching each other literally from head to toe, kissing deeply. Julie shifts her weight and opens her legs and begins slowly rotating her hips in a circular motion. She sits up on Kat then leans back, and before Kat can even figure out what's happening, she realizes they are scissoring with their clits now locked together. She begins to rotate her hips to match Julie's rhythm, pulling Julie's leg tighter against her while Julie does the same on the other end of the bed, careful to avoid Kat's bruised knee. Their hips rise off the bed as they grind into each other, slowly and methodically. They pick up speed, but only a little, both savoring the intense arousal the clit-on-clit action is causing. "Just like that," urges Julie as the two rotate their hips and grind harder and harder against each other.

Once again, Kat starts to feel the tingling sensation of an oncoming orgasm. The sound of her own blood coursing through her ears accompanies her rapid breathing as she moves in unison with Julie. "Oh my God, Julie. I'm coming! You're making me come so hard," Kat cries. Julie orgasms first, but only a second faster and Kat can feel the juices from their bodies intermingling. Kat relaxes on the bed only to be struck by a second, sharp orgasm that causes her to cry out so loudly Cooper starts barking in the living room.

Exhausted, they flop back on the bed, their heads at opposite ends of the mattress. Kat finds the strength to turn herself over so she can, at least, look at Julie, who is staring up at the ceiling, her face still flushed. Kat rests her head on Julie's stomach, holding her there for as long as she can before she starts to hear and feel the rumble of Julie's stomach.

"It sounds like a freight train in here," Kat says with a chuckle.

"It feels like a freight train in there," Julie responds, stroking Kat's hair. "But I really don't want to move."

"Me neither," Kat says. "But if I'm going to have my way with you again, I'll need to keep your energy up. What do you say we go out for brunch? I know the perfect place."

"Hmm. Leave here? That's a big decision."

"The best Bloody Mary on the planet," Kat says, trying to tempt her.

"That's a mighty claim, but Kat, before we get up,

I have to say something to you."

Kat scoots up the bed so they are eye to eye. "What is it?"

"I love you," Julie says sweetly. "And Happy Birthday."

"Oh, baby, I love you more," says Kat, cupping Julie's face with her hands, kissing her deeply. "How on earth did you remember that it's my birthday?"

"I remember everything," she says confidently.

Chapter Thirty-three

Kat sits across from Julie at Chach Restaurant in Provincetown. It's a Sunday morning and the place is pretty full, mostly with locals. Kat comes here often so the waitstaff knows her well. The diner isn't fancy but the food is heavenly, with everything scratch made.

Kat doesn't even bother with a menu. "Do you like oysters?" she asks Julie, as she watches Julie study the menu.

"Yeah, I love them. Why?"

"You can put your menu away. I've got this."

Julie laughs, doing as Kat says.

The waitress arrives at the table, a cute woman with short white blond spiked hair. "Hey, Kat. What can I get you today?"

"Hey, Judy. Two bloodies to start. And you know what I'm going to ask."

"I already checked. It's your lucky day. We have enough for two more orders."

"Perfect. You read my mind. Thanks!"

"You got it," says Judy as she rushes off.

"She's cute." Julie quirks a brow.

"She is," Kat says. "But I'm not interested."

"Why not?"

"Because I'm already in love with a beautiful blonde."

"Ahh, that's what I want to hear!" Julie says,

grinning.

Judy returns with two very large Bloody Marys. "Enjoy," she says as she moves off.

"Wow, this thing is loaded with a full salad serving." Julie removes a toothpick jammed with olives and peppers. "In addition to it being your birthday, which of course I remember, what else are we toasting?"

Kat thinks about this for a second. "To a future together."

"That sounds perfect"—Julie clinks her glass to Kat's—"but can we talk about what that future will look like?" She takes a sip of the Bloody Mary. "I don't want to get ahead of ourselves here. I know we still have some stuff to work out. And I don't want you to think I've got the U-Haul ready to rent, although I do have pretty much everything I own already in my Jeep, so there's that. Oh and this Bloody Mary is amazing."

"Well, what is it you want? Honestly. And I told you it was amazing. Wait until you taste the oysters Benedict. They will blow your mind."

"Honestly? Well, honestly, I want you. I want you to be happy and fulfilled, wherever that is. I want to play basketball for as long as I can in the WNBA. I know there's more money overseas, but I don't really like being out of the country for so long. I could take it or leave it overseas, and I find that playing all year takes too big a toll on my body, anyway. I want to spend some time at home in Utah with my parents when I can. I want to spend more time at the beach. And I did always want a dog."

Kat is thoughtful as she listens to Julie outline her needs, a little surprised to hear Julie say she doesn't care about playing overseas.

"Are you sure?" Kat asks, without a hint of

insecurity. "Because, Julie, you are so young. When I was your age, I had absolutely nothing figured out. It would be okay with me if you said you needed time to experience things, sow your oats, that sort of thing."

Julie tilts hear head to one side, knitting her blond eyebrows together in a frown. "Kat, age has nothing to do with this. I am in love with you. Whatever I experience in life, I want you by my side. Yours are the only oats I want to sow."

Kat smiles at her play on words, sipping her Bloody Mary.

"What do you want?"

"Some things I'm sure about and some things I'm not so sure about," Kat says.

"So let's start with what you are sure about," Julie responds.

"Well, I'm sure about my feelings for you. And I'm sure I love you and I want to be with you in whatever form that takes," Kat says simply. "But I'm not so sure about what I want professionally. I love it here. The thought of leaving to travel all over just to ref games isn't appealing to me anymore, although I miss being around the game. I still haven't figured that part out yet. I don't want you to feel pressured to be here in Provincetown just to be with me when I know you have so much going on. Honestly, the more I think about everything, the more jumbled up I get."

"Okay. Well, look. Can we just agree to take this slow and take it one decision at a time?"

"Yes," Kat says with a sigh of relief.

Judy returns to the table setting down two heaping plates of oysters Benedict. Julie wastes absolutely no time digging in. Kat watches her take the first bite, as Julie closes her eyes, savoring the bite.

"Oh my God, I think I'm having a food orgasm," Julie says with a full mouth.

"Um hmm. I told you," Kat says mid-mouthful. "But don't get too exhausted with this meal because I know of some other kinds of orgasms you're going to have later."

Julie's eyes flash at the suggestion. "No, seriously. If I was on death row, this would be my final meal," continues Julie.

"Duly noted," says Kat.

〜〜〜〜〜

Later that evening, Kat and Julie are wrapped once again in each other's arms, naked in bed after several intense hours of lovemaking.

"Do you ever think about trying to find your dad," Julie asks.

"I used to," Kat replies. "But not so much anymore. I wish I knew him. I wish we had a relationship, but we don't. I honestly don't even know if he's dead or alive, but at this point in my life, there really isn't much of a difference between the two for me." She shifts her body so she can run her hands down Julie's entire back. "So you know all about my wonderful childhood. What about you? Were you this cute little blond tomboy that I imagine running around, wreaking havoc?"

"Basically, yeah, I was. I grew up outside of Brigham City. My dad and mom both worked for Thiokol, a company that makes rocket boosters for the space shuttle. My parents met in high school—you know the story, the head cheerleader marries the star football player. They lived in Utah their whole lives. Both came from big families so we always had aunts and uncles and cousins at the house."

She continues, "My older brother Rob and I basically grew up running around our old farmhouse and barn, riding horses, and playing basketball. And before you ask, because everyone does, we aren't in the Church of Jesus Christ of the Latter-Day Saints, thank God. That would be a huge problem with the whole gay thing. We were one of the like five Catholics in the area, although neither of my parents was very big on church."

"I didn't know you have a brother," Kat says. "I always wanted an older brother to take care of me."

"Had." Julie bites her lip then adds, "Rob died in Afghanistan. He joined the Marines right out of high school and was killed in a roadside bomb on his second tour of duty."

"Oh, Julie, I'm so sorry."

Julie reaches over to the nightstand and pulls out her cell phone. After a few seconds, she hands the phone to Kat, showing her a photo of her and Rob, with Rob proudly wearing his dress uniform.

"Wow. He was so handsome."

"He was. He was such a good brother. Some of my friends had older brothers growing up who always tortured them, but not Rob. He was the one who taught me how to shoot a jump shot properly." Julie's lips turn up at the memory. In her imitation brotherly voice, she continues, "If my sister wants to play basketball, she's going to be the best damned player on the court."

"Sometimes, when I'd get picked on for being a tomboy, Rob would beat up the kid responsible for the wisecracks. He was always there to protect me and make me feel safe. After he died, well, both my parents really struggled. We all did." She pauses and inhales deeply. "We couldn't even see his body when they returned it from Afghanistan because it was so badly damaged." Sadness creeps into her voice. "The only positive thing that came from my brother's death was that my parents didn't care at all when I told them I was gay. They suffered so much loss already that they refused to lose a daughter because I liked girls."

Kat doesn't know what to say to Julie. Her loss is unimaginable to her. She just wraps her up tighter and holds her closer. Julie relaxes into Kat's embrace. "I miss him so much. He never got to see me play in the WNBA," she says with a sigh, "because he died when I blew out my knee. I wasn't sure if I was ever going to play again."

"I'm sure he was somewhere looking down on you, very proud," Kat says.

"I don't know. Do you believe that? Do you really believe after we die we stick around to watch the people we left behind?" Julie asks.

"I'd like to believe my mom is sober and happy and that she sees how I am living my life and that I try to be a good person," Kat muses, absently stroking Julie's back with her thumb.

"Mmm, yeah. I don't know. I would hope Rob is out doing something he loved like riding motorcycles or camping in the mountains."

"Thank you for telling me," says Kat, kissing her gently. "I want to know everything about you. Everything."

"That's going to take some time." Julie nibbles on Kat's earlobe, making her stomach flip.

"I'm in no rush," Kat whispers as she rolls on top of her.

⚝ ⚝ ⚝ ⚝

Two weeks later, Kat sits on her couch covered by a throw blanket with Cooper curled up beside her. She sips a cup of tea, listening to The Weepies "Take it From Me." Her body is relaxed and satiated after two of the most erotic and sexual weeks of her life, filled with such emotion and laughter. Kat knows she could survive a lifetime with those memories although she's very much looking forward to making more.

Her thoughts turn for a moment to Antonia. She hopes Antonia is happy in Cleveland and sends out a silent wish of thanks to her. Kat knows Antonia helped heal a broken part of her and she will always be grateful to her for that.

Julie left this morning for Utah to visit her parents, and as much as Kat savored every second Julie was here, she needs the space to think about what she wants to do, and she's glad for the personal time to do it.

Abby reduced the hours of the gallery substantially, so Kat only has to work a few days a week. The gallery will close up for the cold winter months after the holidays and won't reopen until April. Abby did ask Kat to help out with some winter photo shoots, explaining that she often gets some of her best shots of the beaches during the winter. "There's something magical about the Provincetown beaches in winter," Abby said. "Something about the angle of the light that you can't find anywhere else."

For Kat, the beaches here are magical all the time, but she knows that doing some occasional work with Abby won't be enough to sustain her. With money a little tighter now, she's concerned about picking up another job to help get her through the winter, if she decides to stay here.

She's already put off calling back the league three times about returning to her old job. As Kat listens to Deb Talan's soothing voice, she looks around her cozy home. Could she leave this? Does she want to leave this? Cooper picks her head up off the couch to look at Kat. Even Kat notices Cooper is a little depressed without Julie. "You two bonded," she says to Cooper, squeezing her ear. "I miss her too."

Kat thinks about calling Molly to talk things over, but she already knows Molly wants her back in New York, and she needs to make this decision for herself.

She's on the precipice of truly walking away from the one thing she's worked so hard to achieve. After all, there are only thirty officials in the WNBA. It's an elite and pretty exclusive club. It's not like the money is outrageous either. She was only earning about twenty-thousand dollars a season in the WNBA and another fifty thousand dollars a season in the Big East, depending entirely on the number of games she could schedule and how expensive her own travel costs were.

She earns admittedly less in Provincetown, but her quality of life is so much better, and her needs are far less. She actually saved a fair amount over the summer months too. No, this isn't about the money. Maybe if it were, the decision would be easier. This is about her heart. Looking down at Cooper snoring softly beside her, her heart speaks to her loud and clear.

Kat hears her phone buzz on the couch next to her. She picks it up to see a text from Julie: "I miss you already. I love you."

Kat texts back: "Ditto" and sets the phone down on the coffee table.

She has no idea how she and Julie will make things work, but she knows that somehow they will figure it out—together this time.

She flips open her laptop and sends a quick email. "It's done Cooper-girl. We're home. For good," says Kat. Cooper flutters her eyes open, not really fazed by Kat's words. "Well, now that we've decided on staying here, want to go for a walk on the beach?" Kat asks and within seconds, Cooper is up and standing at the door, her tail wagging. "Yes, this is home now," says Kat, zipping her windbreaker. She gave Julie the biggest piece of her heart, but it was Provincetown that stole the rest.

Chapter Thirty-four

K at blows her whistle and calls out the foul. "Number twenty-four, that's two-four on the arm, two shots." After the table records the foul, she jogs over to the baseline as the players line up and the other official bounces the ball on the free-throw line.

Lower Cape High School is fairly crowded for the girls' varsity basketball team's final home game of the season against Wellfleet High School. The twenty-sixth of February is cold and damp. The Whalers' home crowd, comprised of students and families, holds up signs for the seniors. It's a typical small-town basketball crowd.

In terms of state playoffs, the game is pretty meaningless. The Whalers had a decent season, but not worthy of a postseason bid, so this is it for the three graduating seniors. None of them will be playing in college.

As the second shot goes up and rolls around the rim, Kat glances over at the gym entrance. A few students and parents hover around the snack table.

The game continues and Kat follows the action up the floor. She stops just over half-court, surveying the play from the foul line up to half-court. After a few sloppy passes and a subsequent turnover, the fast break coming toward her shifts her position to the left wing. She looks up at the clock as it rolls down to three, two, one. The buzzer sounds, indicating halftime. Lower

Cape holds a slim 22–17 lead over Wellfleet. The players jog off to the locker rooms while Kat sits on one of the benches near center court, toweling off and downing some water.

It's taken her some time to get used to calling high school basketball again. First, there are only two officials, not three, so she has to cover much more of the court. Second, it took her a while to remember how to let certain calls go at the high school level in order to keep play moving along. It's not exactly challenging for her, but it's enjoyable and means some extra cash and that's all that really matters.

A father of one of the players sits down next to Kat, offering her a Gatorade, which she happily accepts.

"So I hear you were a ref in the WNBA?" the dad asks.

"Yep, that's right. I worked in the league for about four seasons and also reffed in the Big East."

"Wow. That's something. We don't get folks like you working with our programs here very often. What made you leave the big time and come here to call our little Cape Cod programs?"

"Oh, well, you know how it is. The beach called my name. I wanted a less complicated life."

"It's really something. My wife always tells me you're the first ref we've ever seen whose calls we always agree with. She wanted me to say thanks and was wondering if you'd ever want to talk with the kids about your experiences? It would be really great for them to hear from you."

"Well, thank you. And sure, I'd be glad to." Kat gives her cell number to the man so he can contact her with a date.

"That's great. Thanks again!" The dad pops up

and heads back into the stands. Kat laughs as she hears him telling the parents around him that she really was a WNBA referee.

She suddenly feels two hands on her shoulders and doesn't even need to turn around. She knows whose hands those are. She leans back and lets Julie massage her shoulders.

"Hey, babe," says Julie.

"Hey! Happy Birthday! You're here early. I thought you were coming in later?"

"I was, but I wanted to catch the love of my life in action as a birthday present to me. You know you really do look sexy in black and white stripes," Julie teases her.

The players make their way out of the locker rooms and onto the floor. A few begin shooting around. One recognizes Julie and begins whispering to her friends, "Hey, that's Julie Stevens. I think she plays for the New York Liberty."

Julie laughs. "I've been spotted."

"You have. Watch out for the guy in the Patriots sweatshirt. He'll ask you to run a clinic for the girls if he finds out who you are," Kat says.

"Um, guy in the Patriots sweatshirt? Could you narrow that down? There are like twenty."

Kat grabs Julie's hand. "I'd give you a birthday kiss now but people would talk and I might lose my job." Kat grins, knowing full well no one would even care. "I can't believe I will have you all to myself for the next two and a half months."

"Listen, I have a lot of work to do while I'm here. Don't think we are going to be lounging around all day. I've got some serious strength conditioning to do, not to mention improving my handle and footwork and keeping my knee healthy," Julie says, smiling broadly.

"Of course, I wouldn't dream of interfering with your workouts, but I am excited to join you for them," Kat says. "Even the horizontal cardio workouts."

Julie laughs, a sound that Kat will never, ever get used to.

The first horn blows.

"Hey, ref, go easy on the personal fouls, huh? Let the kids play," Julie says, as Kat tosses her towel and water to her and jogs back out on the floor, popping the whistle in her mouth.

"Let's go, ladies," Kat yells to the Wellfleet bench, breaking up their huddle. "Let's get this game moving." Kat tries to focus on the game, pushing aside the butterflies in her stomach at the mere thought of the sheer bliss that awaits her when she gets home with Julie.

෴෴෴

After the game ends and the players and families file out of the gym, Kat's eyes dance as Julie strolls over to her with a basketball held casually under one arm.

"You want to shoot around?" Kat asks.

"You know I do, ref," Julie says.

"I'm not sure they will let us stay, though. I've learned these gyms are crazy about the insurance issues."

"Don't worry, it's all taken care of. I got permission. I pulled the All-Star WNBA card and got a free pass for as long as we want. They'll even let me work out here on my own. They just told me to shut off the lights before we leave. Apparently, I am very trustworthy."

"Really? Hmm. Alone with you in the gym? This could be more interesting than I thought." Kat winks, already aroused at the thought of making love to Julie on a basketball court.

"Get your mind out of the gutter. I just want to play a friendly game." Julie shakes her head at Kat and starts dribbling the ball around her back and in between her legs with the extreme ease and confidence of a professional player.

"Oh yeah? And what kind of game are we playing? P-I-G?"

"No, I'm thinking something with more letters. I don't want to be gypped by a short game, after all," Julie says playfully as she takes a quick jumper at the foul line that is nothing but net.

"Okay. How about H-O-R-S-E?"

"No, still too short," Julie yells as she tracks down the ball and dribbles out to the wing to take another jumper, again all net.

"Listen, you're warming up here with all this stalling and I haven't taken a shot yet. How about you share the ball and tell me what we're playing for?"

Julie strolls over to Kat and hands her the ball. "How about M-A-R-R-Y-M-E?" she asks as she drops to one knee, holding a diamond ring in front of her.

Kat stares at Julie in utter disbelief. She starts to say something in response but no sound comes out. She looks down at Julie, kneeling at center court and can't believe here, of all places, is where Julie decides to pop the question.

"Katherine Elizabeth Schaefer, will you marry me?

"Yes. A thousand times yes. Of course!" Kat shouts as she holds out her hand for Julie to slide the ring on her finger. Kat drops the basketball and the sound of it bouncing echoes in the empty gym. Julie stands and Kat wraps Julie in a tight embrace, never wanting to let go of this moment.

Finally, Julie breaks free. Both have tears streaming

down their faces. "Oh my God, I can't wait to tell Molly! She's going to die when she finds out we now have two weddings to plan."

"Tell her now. She's right over there." Julie points to the entrance where Kat sees Molly and Joanne and Molly's parents. Mrs. O'Brien dabs her eyes with a tissue but Mr. O'Brien is openly crying and smiling at the same time. Molly waves at Kat while holding up a cell phone to capture the moment.

Kat takes Julie's face in her hands and kisses her. "Thank you," she whispers. "This is perfect. I love you so much. We need to get you a ring too!"

"I love you too. I don't need a ring. But there is this framed photograph of a gorgeous woman at the beach hanging in a Provincetown gallery that I've had my eye on. Now get over there before Molly has a heart attack."

Kat runs over to Molly and hugs her tightly. "You don't think I'd miss this do you? After all, I am taking total and complete credit for this. If I didn't pull that little spy game and steal Julie's number off your cell, none of this would have happened," Molly says with a wink.

"Oh, honey! We are so happy for you. Aren't we, Paddie?" Mrs. O'Brien says, beaming as they all take turns hugging Kat and Julie. Everyone laughs as they see strong, ex-police officer Patrick O'Brien crying like a schoolgirl, unable to do anything more than nod in agreement.

"Oh, I swear, that man is such a mush." Mrs. O'Brien chuckles.

"So when is the wedding?" Joanne asks.

"Well, April seems to be the perfect month before the season starts," Julie says, "although we haven't exactly talked about it yet."

"Oh my God, two weddings in one month, Paddy. I am going on such a diet!"

Kat finds Julie's hand and squeezes it tightly.

"April is perfect," she says, looking deeply into Julie's eyes.

Epilogue

The New York Liberty tip off their sixteenth season in franchise history with a home game at Madison Square Garden against the Atlanta Dream on Sunday, June 5, 2011.

As the lights go out in the Garden and the starting lineups are announced, Kat can't help but feel the excitement in the air and her own nervousness about the game.

The strobe lights circle the darkened arena as the pregame video plays. Kat looks up at the center court monitor, high above, watching the video that is bound to pump up the Liberty players since they are seeing it too for the first time this season. As the light comes on in the arena, the announcer begins: "And now, announcing your two thousand and eleven New York Liberty." The crowd cheers. "At guard, from the University of Connecticut, number fifteen, Julie Stevens!"

This is the first professional game Kat has ever attended where she is sitting in the stands and is not on the floor working the game. She realizes she can actually cheer for Julie openly now, so she claps her hands together. Julie jogs to center court and looks right at Kat, smiling broadly. "I love you," she silently mouths to Kat. Turning her head to view the sideline, Kat sees Deb standing with the other two officials. Deb winks at Kat, and Kat smiles back.

As the rest of the Liberty starting lineup is

announced, Kat takes in the whole experience and sees the game for the first time as entertainment. She knows this will be a great game.

Kat nudges Molly next to her. "I can't believe that's my wife out there."

"It's surreal—we are both married ladies," Molly says, nudging her back.

"I never noticed how absolutely freezing it is in here!" Kat wraps her arms across her chest.

Molly and Kat look at each other, laughing, and yell in unison their favorite *Beaches* movie quote of all time, "Send the heat up!"

The buzzer sounds for the game to begin.

About the Author

Lucy J. Madison is a writer who grew up in rural Connecticut, developing an intense love of nature, animals, and the beach at a very early age. She is a former standout college basketball player and avid outdoorswoman. Lucy received a Master of Arts in Liberal Studies from Wesleyan University and is the recipient of numerous writing awards. She resides with her wife in Connecticut and in Provincetown, MA along with their beloved pets.

You can contact Lucy at -

www.lucyjmadison.com
Twitter @lucyjmadison

Check out other Sapphire Authors

Forever Faithful by Isabellla
ISBN - 978-1-939062-75-8

Life is what happens when you make other plans, and Nic and Claire have just found out that life and the Marine Corps have other plans for their lives.

Nic Caldwell has served her country, met the woman of her dreams, and has reached the rank of Lieutenant Colonel. She's studying at one of the nation's most prestigious military universities, setting her sights on a research position after graduation. Things couldn't be better and then it happens; a sudden assignment to Afghanistan derails any thoughts of marriage and wedded bliss. Another combat zone, another tragedy, and Nic suddenly finds herself fighting for her life.

Claire Monroe loves her new life in Monterey. She's finally where she wants to be, getting ready to start her master's program at the local university, watching her daughter, Grace, growing up, and getting ready to marry the love of her life. What could possibly derail a perfect life? The Marine Corps.

Will Nic survive Afghanistan? Can Claire step up and be the strength in their relationship? Or will this overseas assignment and a catastrophic accident divide their once happy home?

CPSIA information can be obtained
at www.ICGtesting.com
Printed in the USA
LVOW11s1724080617

537418LV00002B/409/P

9 781943 353255